Lina lay there, sti...
bathed in the streetlight that...
through the sheet. She didn't mind being
awake in the least.

The world hadn't felt so right in a very long while
and she didn't want to miss a moment, for it felt
too good to be true.

Too good to last?

She listened to the swish of cars below and the soft
sound of Garth asleep by her side.

She wanted to reach out and touch his flat stomach,
to wake him up in the nicest of ways. She was
smiling to herself at the thought of that as she
looked at his gorgeous features.

But then it happened again, that flash of
recognition: she knew him. Lina was sure of it.

Oh, where had she seen that profile before?

She had felt it that first night they'd met, when
she'd walked into the staff room and seen him
sleeping upright in a chair—a jolt of recognition
had shot through her.

And now it was happening again.

The straight aquiline nose, lips slightly parted…

It was like trying to recall a dream.

Dear Reader,

Welcome to my fictional COVID-free world. :)

I thought long and hard about what to include, then decided that if I'd had enough of COVID, then so might my wonderful readers, and so it isn't mentioned at all. Hopefully this Dear Reader letter dates my book in the nicest of ways and we're all back to normal by the time you read this! I know that I want cafés and long lunches, as well as spontaneous kisses and to tumble into bed after staring too long at gorgeous lips, and that's what happens here…

And, may I say, emergency consultant Garth Hughes has exceptionally sexy lips that haven't smiled very much for the past six years. He really needed someone like paramedic Lina Edwards to bring joy and passion back into his life. This, Lina did until life caught up in a way neither could have anticipated…

Their story made me cry a lot while I wrote it, but it made me laugh, too, so it's a case of pass the tissues rather than the hand sanitizer.

I hope Garth and Lina's story gives you a little break during difficult times.

Happy reading!

C xxxx

UNLOCKING THE DOCTOR'S SECRETS

———

CAROL MARINELLI

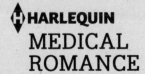

HARLEQUIN

MEDICAL
ROMANCE

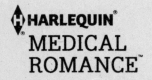

HARLEQUIN®
MEDICAL
ROMANCE™

Recycling programs
for this product may
not exist in your area.

ISBN-13: 978-1-335-40875-4

Unlocking the Doctor's Secrets

Copyright © 2021 by Carol Marinelli

Harlequin Enterprises ULC
22 Adelaide St. West, 40th Floor
Toronto, Ontario M5H 4E3, Canada
www.Harlequin.com

Printed in U.S.A.

Carol Marinelli recently filled in a form asking for her job title. Thrilled to be able to put down her answer, she put "writer". Then it asked what Carol did for relaxation and she put down the truth—"writing." The third question asked for her hobbies. Well, not wanting to look obsessed, she crossed her fingers and answered "swimming"—but, given that the chlorine in the pool does terrible things to her highlights, I'm sure you can guess the real answer!

Books by Carol Marinelli

Harlequin Medical Romance

Ruthless Royal Sheikhs

Captive for the Sheikh's Pleasure
(Available from Harlequin Presents)
Christmas Bride for the Sheikh

Paddington Children's Hospital

Their One Night Baby

Playboy on Her Christmas List
Their Secret Royal Baby
The Midwife's One-Night Fling
The Nurse's Reunion Wish

Harlequin Presents

Those Notorious Romanos

Italy's Most Scandalous Virgin
The Italian's Most Forbidden Virgin

Visit the Author Profile page
at Harlequin.com for more titles.

PROLOGUE

'You'll be nursing here tomorrow night!'

From the ambulance bay, Lina Edwards looked towards the bright lights of The Primary Hospital. She was now back in the driving seat after completing the handover for a patient they had just blue lighted.

'At least I'll be warm.'

It was a wet and cold Thursday night, and they really hadn't stopped since the start of their shift. Brendan held her coffee while Lina re-tied her long, damp black hair and tried to both dry off and warm up as they took a moment for a welcome break after a long and busy night.

As well as being a paramedic, Lina was also a registered nurse and did the occasional shift in Accident and Emergency, not just to keep her registration current but also to keep her hand in. 'You might be here too,' she pointed out to her colleague. Brendan's wife, Alison, was booked to have their first baby here. 'Or rather you might be up on Maternity!'

'Fingers crossed that it won't be for another three weeks,' Brendan said, 'although I swear that Alison's in labour.'

'You've been saying that for the past fortnight.' Lina smiled as she opened up the foil on her egg mayonnaise sandwiches.

'God, not them again,' Brendan groaned, and wound down the window a touch. 'If it isn't eggs then it's tuna.'

'What have you got?' Lina asked, because, well, they always asked, and food was an especially big topic at the moment given that Brendan was on a diet and trying to lose weight.

'A salad wrap, a tub of cottage cheese and an orange,' he sighed, checking his phone for the umpteenth time. 'She was on edge this evening before I left for work.'

'I'm sure Alison would call if anything was happening. There wasn't a light on when we drove past.'

'True.'

Their ambulance station was west of London but of course they went where their shift led them and sometimes they ended up at The Primary, a huge general hospital in the north of London, close to where Brendan and Alison lived and Lina once had.

'I wonder who I'll end up working with tomorrow,' Brendan mused. 'I hope it's not Peter.'

'Perfect Peter,' Lina groaned, because there was a good chance that she'd be working with him when Brendan went on paternity leave and Pedantic Peter could also be Peter's nickname. 'Well, if you do end up with him, just remember that it's only temporary *and* that it's overtime.'

'I certainly need it.'

'Me too,' Lina agreed. 'This shift tomorrow is going to help pay for my next trip.'

'Another one?'

Lina nodded. She loved nothing more than to get away. It was the time she got to not just let down her guard but to think… or not. Her relationship with her family was complex, her flatmate was wonderful but always *there* and as well as that her work was stressful—it required a series of rapid decisions and being assertive, while at other times a lot of aimless killing time, as they were doing now.

Walking, wherever her train or coach ticket took her, replenished Lina. But there was another reason she had been away so much lately—she was seriously considering relocating from London and was quietly working out her options, not that she had told anyone. Soon, though, she would have no choice but to share the news. These days she was all too often on the phone with the bank and estate agents and Brendan had noticed. Aside from that, she had applied for a job in Newcastle and needed a preliminary reference.

'I've been thinking…' Brendan said as he peered into his salad wrap as if hoping some ham and cheese might miraculously appear.

'About what?'

'Your love life.'

'I have no love life,' Lina said. 'So you can save your grey matter, I really am through. Men are a mystery and one I have no wish to solve—I've decided that I'm sticking with Gretel…' Gretel was her needy and demanding ancient diabetic cat.

'Please.'

'I mean it,' Lina said. 'It's been months since I've been on a date and I intend to keep it that way. I'm just sick of…' Her voice trailed off and she looked over at Brendan, wondering if now was the time to tell him the plans she had in mind.

'Sick of what?'

'I don't know,' Lina said, deciding against

telling him just yet—she knew Brendan would try to dissuade her and so instead she spoke of other things on her mind—men, or the lack of decent, single ones. 'Being dumped, being let down, being left sitting alone in a restaurant while he makes his escape...'

They had worked together for more than two years and so Brendan knew about her rather disastrous love life, in the same way she knew about his and Alison's difficult journey with IVF and the upcoming birth of their baby.

He didn't know all of it, though.

Lina wasn't sure if it was bad luck or poor judgement that plagued her, but at twenty-nine she didn't have so much as a long relationship to her name, let alone a broken engagement, or anything of note really. Just awful dates or, what she considered even worse, wonderful dates, followed by more dates, and bed—except, just as she got her hopes up, she'd find out he was cheating, or he failed to call, or it all just petered out, or she was told she was too abrupt, too work obsessed, not feminine enough...

'I don't think there are any good guys left,' she admitted.

'Of course there are. You just go into

things expecting to be let down. We're not all like your dad, Lina…'

And though Brendan was trying to say the right thing, even that annoyed her—not that she let it show.

Oh, her friends all knew about her father's leaving and moving overseas, they just didn't know the friable scar it had left on her heart—one that bled on contact. Lina kept her deepest feelings well tucked away. Everyone carelessly assumed that she must be angry with her father for leaving them to live in Singapore, when the truth was that she simply missed him, and still, to this day, wondered what she had done wrong. How someone who had supposedly loved her could simply get up and leave and make so little effort to keep in touch.

But instead of telling Brendan the truth she offered a blithe response about her dating life, one she had almost come to believe. 'I just can't be doing with it all…'

'You should try online dating.' Brendan suggested, but she shook her head even as he persisted with the idea. 'That's how Alison and I met.'

'I never knew that!'

'Best thing I ever did.'

But Lina wasn't convinced. While it was

true that he and Alison were utterly devoted, Brendan seemed to think that just because it had worked out so spectacularly for himself and Alison, true love was a mere swipe away.

'I did try it,' Lina admitted as she gazed out through the windscreen. The clouds had parted and she looked out at the blue hour, the delicious navy sky that crept in just before dawn. 'Several times.' She gave a tired laugh as she thought of the hours of preparation her beautician flatmate had taken to deem her suitable for a date—her pale skin had been fake tanned, her wavy hair straightened and smoothed, her green eyes framed with fake eyelashes and eyeliner and the photo had been taken at an angle that supposedly slimmed... 'Shona got me all tarted up for my photo.'

'You never said.'

'No, because it didn't work out. I got loads of responses but it would seem I'm a bit of a let-down in the ample flesh.'

'Well, then, put up a picture of yourself as you...'

'I tried that too,' Lina sighed, thinking of the real picture she had put up of herself, dressed in walking gear sitting on top of a snow-capped hill, feeling relaxed and accomplished and at peace. '*She's* nowhere near as popular, at least not with anyone I find attractive.'

It was a fact.

The type of men she liked seemed to like the type of woman she wasn't.

Lina spent most of her life at work and in overalls and steel toecap boots. On her days off she liked nothing better than to take a coach or train and go walking and exploring. There was no real reason for make-up, let alone heels and glamorous outfits, and anyway she felt stupid in them.

She had been raised on her brother's cast-offs and the only real concession that she was female had been that her mother had trimmed her long black hair now and then, rather than taking the clippers to it like she had for her brothers. The only sexy clothing she possessed was her vast collection of *gorgeous* colourful underwear—not that she would be discussing that with Brendan!

'Men *say* that they like independent women…'

'They do,' Brendan assured her, 'though you are a bit bossy…'

'I'm assertive,' Lina corrected. Well, at least she was at work. 'Have a sandwich if you want one.'

'Assertive, then,' Brendan agreed as he took a sandwich. 'Forthright.'

And she was, except what Brendan didn't know was that it was a learned trait.

She had been so sensitive growing up.

Every tease from her brothers had felt like a bee sting, and her mum, whom Lina adored, could be described as tactless at best. The only person who had understood her finely tuned ways had been her dad. Well, she could remember long walks, when her mother and brothers had chosen to stay on the beach or back at the holiday house they'd rented, and she'd tell her dad about trouble at school, or a friend that had turned out not to actually be one...

It had broken her heart when he'd left and since then her walls had gone up.

But that sensitive edge had surfaced again during her nursing training. She'd often considered quitting, and though she'd loved paramedicine, during her grad year as a paramedic on several occasions it had hurt too much and she'd considered simply walking away.

Well could Lina remember a wretched shift, going from a disaster into the mundane and just wanting to pause a moment and cry. She had gone to her mum's, hoping for wise words and comfort—not exactly her mother's forte. Instead, after a brief break when she'd taken a few days off to wander the countryside and gather her thoughts, she'd realised that if she seriously wanted to pursue paramedicine as a career then she had to toughen the hell up—at least on a surface level.

The tough, assertive, wickedly funny Lina had sort of become the norm—except that the tough, assertive, wickedly funny Lina everyone knew wasn't entirely her.

'My last date said I spoke about work too much,' Lina admitted.

'Alison says it's all I talk about too,' Brendan said, and Lina couldn't help but laugh.

'What's so funny?'

'At work *all* you talk about is Alison and the baby...'

'Guilty as charged,'

As Brendan smiled fondly, Lina felt a wave of...not envy, more pensiveness. She didn't mind a bit that he talked about the wonderful Alison all the time—in fact, it rather restored her faith in men.

Close to thirty, Lina was more than a little jaded as she examined her dating past with her colleague. 'The one before complained when I changed his tyre when he got a flat. He said I emasculated him.'

'Ha-ha,' Brendan said.

'I don't really have interests. Well, it's not as if I go to the gym…'

'You have your walking.'

'Yes.' Lina said, 'but I do it so lazily. Remember that guy I met who turned out to be a racewalker! That date nearly killed me!'

Brendan laughed.

'I like food, but even that's complicated. I'm not a foodie…'

'You like cakes and puddings…'

'And sandwiches,' Lina added, 'but only particular combinations.'

'You like antique shops,' Brendan reminded her. 'Though maybe leave that out of your online bio, or you'll be attracting the oldies.'

'Oh, I already do!' Lina sighed.

'Wear a bit of make-up now and then, have wine instead of beer…'

'Careful,' Lina warned.

'Be more agreeable…' He was really teasing her now. 'Ask him if he'd like his slippers warmed…' He turned and smiled. 'Just be yourself, Lina.'

Which was all well and good in theory, except *herself* didn't seem to be getting very far! And she was about to quip the same, but there really was something about the blue hour, that slice of time before dawn, that made you delve a little deeper.

Maybe it was that Brendan had become such a good friend.

Or perhaps she was just tired, but for whatever reason Lina admitted a deeper truth. 'I think it would be harder...'

'What?' Brendan frowned.

'Being completely yourself, only to then have them leave. It's better to hold a part of yourself back.'

Brendan, as he ate her last egg sandwich, respectfully disagreed.

CHAPTER ONE

'WHAT DOCTOR'S ON TONIGHT?'

As he made a mug of tea from the kitchenette beside the staffroom, consultant Garth Hughes could hear the night team chatting away.

'Huba,' said May, the nurse in charge, referring, in her thick Irish brogue, to one of the junior doctors. 'I just saw her in the changing room.'

'Desmond until midnight and Garth through till morning,' someone else chimed in. 'He's back from his leave.'

'Well, hopefully the break has put him in a more cheerful mood,' May said, and then, because she'd just seen him in the kitchen, added loudly. 'And I'd say it to his face if he were here.'

'I know you would, May,' Garth responded as he squeezed out his teabag with a wry smile and then took his mug into the crowded staffroom.

He glanced around for a seat and took one of the few available.

'Well, has it?' May pushed, but then forgot about the consultant on call tonight, clearly delighted by who had just walked in. 'Lina!' She gave a bright smile. 'I was hoping that we'd get you.'

'I thought I was going to be late...' she said, and as he stirred his tea Garth glanced up at the new arrival.

She *looked* late.

Her long dark hair was untied and she was wrapping a stethoscope round her neck and clipping on a lanyard, as well as seeming a little breathless and just...rushing. 'I promised to drop in on Mum and she wouldn't stop talking and then when I got here I couldn't find the scrubs...'

'They've been moved,' Dianne said. 'The surgeons keep pinching them so they're behind the lockers...'

'I know that now,' Lina said as she took a seat next to Garth and bent over to do her runners up. 'But I felt like the new girl having to ask where they were...'

'You're never the new girl,' May said. 'How's Mum?'

'Off out on a hot date,' Lina replied. 'I had to do her roots. She tells them she's mid-forties.'

'If I remember rightly she was mid-forties when you did your training.' May laughed and then added for the benefit of anyone who didn't know, 'Lina did her placements here.'

It was as much of an introduction as anyone really got—the roster was so big and fluid that there were new faces all the time, except it was clear to Garth that, though in his six months at The Primary he'd never come across her, Lina was something of a regular.

Still, the new addition to the room was quickly forgotten by all as May resumed her grilling of him.

'Well, has it?' May said, and looked at directly at Garth.

'Sorry?' He was more than used to a break in the conversation and May's ability to pick up from where she'd left off, but unusually he was completely unable to recall what they'd been talking about before Lina had arrived.

The new addition's arrival *hadn't* been forgotten by all. In fact, Garth was by far too aware of her.

She took up too much space.

Well, she barely touched him, but she'd moved on from doing up her runners to pulling her long black hair into a ponytail and was just this fidgeting ball beside him, filling up his senses, flooding them with newly washed hair and then the sound of a fizzy pop as she opened a can of soft drink and took a sip.

'That's better,' she said, completely to herself—except he had to actively resist responding.

Yes, it was hard to focus as she tapped little chinks of awareness into his usually impervious shield. He checked himself and tried to get back to whatever it was they'd been discussing before this woman who took up too much headroom had taken a seat beside him. 'You've lost me, May,' Garth admitted. 'What did you say?'

'Has the time off put you in a better mood?'

'Of course,' he responded wryly. Garth knew that May was half teasing and half delving.

He'd hoped the break would improve things, and for a while it had, but there had been grey skies and a steady drizzle of rain on his drive back from Wales that had matched his mood exactly. The days were still short and so by the time he had arrived back at his flat it had been dark, and the place that had been bought to provide a new start had felt nothing but cold and empty.

Or was it that *he* felt cold and empty?

It really was a case of one foot forward and ten steps back, but then trips to Wales always did that to him.

'How *was* your break?' Dianne asked.

'Fine.' Garth answered, when in truth the last part had been hell.

A necessary hell, though.

'You had two weeks off, didn't you?'

God, why didn't they let it drop? Garth thought to himself. Yet, conversely, he knew he'd be the first to ask about a colleague's holiday, or how their weekend off had been. As well as that, he'd promised he would make more effort, really give his all to this new start, and so he answered, 'Yes, two weeks.'

'Where did you go?' May joined in the rather one-sided conversation. 'What did you do with yourself? Did you catch up with your family?'

He was tempted to answer honestly, not because he wanted the sympathy, more for the bliss of the silence that would inevitably follow, but instead he deflected. 'No.' Garth gave a shake of his head. 'There just wasn't time. To tell you the truth, I was busy with...'

His voice lowered and he leaned forward a little, as if about to share a secret, and May eagerly leaned forward too, clearly delighted that the very private Garth was about to reveal more of himself. 'Did I tell you that I booked in to have a personality transplant during my leave, in the hope I'd suddenly start sharing with all of you the ins and outs of my private life?' There was the sound of laughter from beside him and clearly Lina got his slightly sarcastic response.

So too did May. 'It didn't take, then.'

'No,' Garth said, 'it didn't take.'

'Oh, well.' May stood up to head out and face the night, as did the rest of the nursing team. 'We'll just have to work with what we've got.'

It was all good-natured teasing, and as the staff, Lina included, stood to leave, he called them back. 'I did bring you these, though.' He placed a ginormous paper bag, all shiny with butter, on the coffee table. 'They're best eaten on the day they were made...'

'What are they?' May asked, picking up the bag and peering into it.

'Welsh cakes.'

'They don't look like cakes.' May frowned as she took one.

'They're called bakestones,' Dianne said as she helped herself to two. 'My gran used to make them for us.'

'Well, I've never heard of them,' May admitted, taking one herself and wrapping it in tissue. 'I'll have one with my next coffee.'

A few others dived in, but he found himself watching as Lina held back, even though she sniffed the air and gave a slight lick of her lips. 'Help yourself,' Garth offered, guessing she wasn't taking one as she wasn't a permanent member of staff.

'Maybe on my break…'

'They'll be gone by then,' Garth said. 'I wouldn't wait if I were you.'

'Well…' Lina said as she took one and wrapped it in a tissue. 'Thanks very much.'

'You're welcome.'

'Don't mind him,' Garth heard May saying to Lina as the nursing staff spread out across the department. 'I'll warn you now, his bark is worse than his bite.'

As their voices faded into the distance, Garth wasn't exactly surprised to hear May's first summing up of him but, yes, it both registered and stung. He'd been determined to come back from his break with a new attitude.

New flat.

New start.

Well, that had been the plan, but instead, when they'd asked about his break, he had fallen at the first hurdle.

May had had a quiet word with him before he'd left.

Well, not a word, more she had asked a pointed question. They'd been drinking tea in May's office, going through the mountain of paperwork that was always piling up, when she'd asked if there was trouble at home.

'Trouble at home?' He'd frowned, wondering where the hell that had come from.

'I'm just asking because when I was going through some difficulties with my son, well, I tended to bring things to work a bit. I never meant to, of course. If there is a problem at home then know that you can speak to me— it would never go any further.'

'May...' He'd given an incredulous smile. How the hell could there be trouble at home when there was no one at home? But then he'd swallowed, realised perhaps that he was being told, albeit kindly, that he wasn't the sunniest to have around. 'There's no trouble at home.'

'Good,' May had said. 'It was just a stab in the dark. I mean, I don't even know if you've a family...' Perhaps she registered his frown. 'Okay, I know a little. I was on the interview panel, Garth...'

He gritted his teeth because, yes, there was a large gap in his résumé that protocol dictated he explain the necessary, but from that point on he had refused to discuss it. 'We don't all put photos up on our desk, May,' he had said tartly, glancing at the array on hers. 'Are there any problems with my work?'

'None,' she'd said. 'You're an excellent doctor.' Which might sound like a compliment except there was no elaboration.

'Is that a backhanded compliment?'

'It's an observation, Garth. You're an excellent doctor, and you're great to work with, but I can't attest to much else because you don't give us anything else to go on.'

May's observation he had taken seriously.

Oh, he wasn't about to open up to May. And there was never going to be any chance of him being all ho-ho-ho, but with the new flat and two weeks' break he had been determined to come back a little more, well, open.

Like Lina.

She remained in his head and that quietly stunned him—and Garth wasn't used to feeling like that.

Aside from the immediate physical attraction to Lina, which was unsettling in itself, were the glaring disparities on display to him. He'd met her for all of two minutes and he already knew more about her life than the entire department knew about his: she had a presumably single mum nearby who lied about her age and dated, and to whom she seemed close, she'd worked at The Primary before and hated feeling like the new girl...

All that gleaned in one breezy conversation, whereas they had to turn the thumbscrews to get information out of him.

Garth knew he was way too remote with them all.

He looked at the stupid cakes, which had been a sort of olive branch, an effort to show that he did appreciate his team.

They knew that, surely?

He told them often enough and he thanked them and debriefed them after difficult cases and *always* had their backs, but, no, he was not going to sit in the staffroom and tell them where he'd been on his days off, or even hint at the hell of the past couple of days.

It was, he had found, far better to leave his private life at home. Except this wasn't a locum position or a temporary role, it was a permanent position, his first since—

Garth closed his eyes.

All these years on and he still could not say it easily, even to himself.

Lina wasn't quite sure who May was talking about as they headed through the unit.

She hoped the conversation was about Garth, because there had been a prickle of awareness between them and she wanted to know more about him, but May's words about his bark being worse than his bite didn't quite correlate with the man who, while a touch distant, had seemed friendly.

'Who?' Lina checked.

'Garth, the consultant on tonight…'

'He seemed okay,' Lina said. 'Mind you, he did give me a biscuit and we all know that I can be bought for food!'

May laughed. 'Have you come across him before?'

'No.' Lina said, casting her mind back. Her work as a paramedic was so variable that sometimes she could be at The Primary twice in a single day, while at other times there might be weeks in between cases. 'I don't think so.'

'He comes across as the most miserable sort—I mean, grumpy doesn't even begin to describe it—unless you're a patient, of course, *then* he's nice. I've a soft spot for him, though.'

'What sort of soft spot?' Lina nudged, making May laugh.

'A motherly soft spot, you cheeky thing. The trouble with Garth is he's not...well, he doesn't *let* himself be one of us. I'm working on it, though.'

It sounded like an odd statement, but Lina knew what May meant. ED could be a cliquey place at times, and though Lina only did the occasional shift, she kept herself *in*—stopping for a chat when she brought in a patient if time allowed, and attending the Christmas do and such. Now that she came to think of it, Garth hadn't been there—his dark good looks would not have gone unnoticed. A case in point: Lina had noticed him tonight the very second she had come into the staffroom.

Even sitting down, he stood out!

His black hair and unshaven scowling face had had her all flustered when she'd seen that the only spare seat was the one next to him.

Even his voice was sexy, with a deep tone and just a hint of an accent behind his well-schooled accent that she hadn't quite placed until he had mentioned the Welsh bake-stones.

Yes, he was Welsh.

'Still, he keeps the place running well,' May added, 'which is all I'm asking for these days. It's good to have you with us for the night, Lina.'

May wasted no time allocating the work when they arrived in Section A. 'You don't need to hear the handover up here, Lina. Can you take Tanya the student and keep Section B open, please? Elise is already down there with the aim of having it closed by midnight...' She peered at the waiting room. 'Though I doubt that's going to happen.'

Section B was for the 'walking wounded', and though Lina would have preferred to be with the main action she was more than happy to go where she was put. Elise and the student were organised and Huba, the junior doctor, clearly knew her stuff, but tended to double-check everything, which rather slowed things down.

'I know you, don't I?' Huba said as she

wrote up a tetanus shot and some antibiotics for a hand injury that Lina was about to dress, but not until *after* Garth came to check the wound. 'Have you worked here before?'

'Not for a while,' Lina said. 'Well, not as a nurse. I think you know me from when we brought in a burns patient a couple of months ago and you were on. I'm a paramedic.'

'Oh, yes.' Her shoulders briefly slumped. 'I do remember you now.'

'Dreadful, wasn't it?' Lina said, but Huba moved the subject away from that night.

'So you're a paramedic *and* a nurse? How does that work?'

'I studied nursing and graduated,' Lina said, 'but my last placement was here in Emergency and I guess that was when I decided that I wanted to be a paramedic…' She didn't get to finish the conversation because Garth had arrived and Huba seemed a bit flustered by that fact.

'Thanks for this, Garth. I just wanted you to check this hand before he goes home. I'm worried that he's not giving us the full story and that it's a human bite.'

'You've put him on antibiotics?' Garth checked as he read through the notes, 'and brought him back to hand clinic for evaluation tomorrow…'

'Yes, but I'd just like you to check for function. I'm worried that there might be a nicked tendon and that he might need admitting.'

Garth took the card and stalked off to the cubicle then turned and looked at Huba. 'Are you coming?'

'Of course.'

They returned just a couple of moments later and he handed Lina the card. 'Huba's right—it is a human bite, not that he's admitting to it. We'll see him in hand clinic tomorrow. Stress again the importance of elevation and that he really needs to come back for review.'

'I will,' Lina said as he glanced around at the thinning-out Section B waiting room.

'And perhaps start to close up here,' Garth said.

Lina started to respond that she was about to, when Huba chimed in. 'May wants it kept open till at least midnight.'

Lina stood up, wearing not quite a frown but a smudge of one, because May *hadn't* said that. In fact, May would like nothing more than Section B to be closed in a timely fashion and all staff working the main section, but of course she wasn't going to correct Huba in front of her senior, so instead she gave a nod to Garth. 'Sure,' she said to his departing back, and she could feel not so much a chill in the air but more a certain tension, and that was confirmed when Huba put down her pen and ran a worried hand over her brow.

'I shouldn't have called him up to check on that hand.'

'Of course you should if you're concerned. And you're right about the human bite—they can turn nasty,' Lina said, though in fairness Huba called Garth up a lot. 'He shouldn't make you feel bad for asking.'

'He doesn't make me feel bad. If anything, he's more than willing to have me run things by him. It's just that I'm always asking these days.' Lina wasn't sure she understood. 'That night of the house fire…' Huba said, and her brown eyes suddenly filled with tears and she shook her head. 'It doesn't matter.'

Clearly it did matter, because Huba went very quiet then, and though curious as to what might have happened, Lina decided it would be unfair to push as Huba clearly didn't want to talk further about it.

It had been a very fraught night, with

three little children fatally injured as well as their mother, and though she couldn't recall Garth being there as she herself had rushed the mother in, perhaps he had been around, and, like a lot of people that night, not at his sunniest.

'If you want to talk…' Lina said, and touched Huba's arm.

'Thank you,' Huba said, but she shook her head. 'I'll be fine.'

'Or a coffee?' she offered.

'I would love one.' Huba smiled.

'That I can do!'

She made Huba a drink and there were still a couple of the Welsh cakes in Garth's bag, so she put them on a plate and brough them around, but even as she put them down for a grateful Huba, the intercom buzzed and May asked if Lina could come now for a patient expected in Resus. 'Now!'

It was bedlam up in Section A, with the cubicles all full and stretchers lined up awaiting admission, where Lina would usually be as a paramedic. She headed straight into a very full resus. There was a red-in-the-face two-year-old screaming and a lot of the staff were with him; as well as that, a crash team was working on a young woman but May urgently signalled her to head to the middle bay. 'We've got a STEMI coming in, the second on cardiac team has been paged, but we're tied up with this amitriptyline OD. It's just you and Garth until they get here.'

A STEMI was a very serious type of heart attack and one in which Lina was well versed and trained. 'Does the cath lab know?' Lina asked, but May was back to concentrating on her own patient now, so Lina ducked into the middle bay.

Garth was there, pulling up drugs, and looked a little less than impressed when he saw that help had arrived in the shape of the casual nurse.

'Where is everyone?' he said. 'The patient that's coming in is time-critical.'

As if she didn't know! Still, Lina bit back a smart response and more suitably replied, 'The first on team are tied up next door.'

'I know that,' Garth retorted. 'I called them.'

'The second on team has been paged,' Lina said, while knowing he really meant where the hell were the nursing staff? 'I'm going to check that Cath Lab knows.'

Thankfully, because all her nursing shifts were done at The Primary, Lina had a list of extension numbers clipped to the back of her lanyard and had soon ensured that all the relevant staff had been alerted. She wheeled back a spare IVAC pump to the bay and was opening packs when the paramedic team wheeled in the grey-faced, barely conscious patient.

Annette, one of the paramedics, did a slight double take when she saw Lina, but now was not the time for a catch-up so instead she handed over the patient.

'Walter James, fifty-eight years old, in London on business, no previous history or allergies...' All this was said while the man was moved from the stretcher to the resuscitation bed.

'Mr James, you're at The Primary,' she said as she attached him to the hospital's own equipment, but he was barely responsive. She started running a twelve-lead ECG as Garth examined the one that the paramedics had brought in as they continued the handover.

'Any family?' Lina asked Annette.

'An ex-wife in Nottingham is all we could glean before his BP dropped.'

Lina looked at the man on the bed. Though she was very tough, things still got to her at times...and this was one of those times.

Still, she pushed all thoughts of her dad and the unfortunate timing of his heart at-

tack out of her mind as the paramedics con-
cluded their handover.

'Thank you,' Garth said to them as he
worked on the patient. 'Excellent work...'

Well, even if he was a bit bearish, the fact
that he thanked the paramedics won Lina
onside. She was so used to being ignored
when they brought in a critically ill patient;
it was a good consultant who actually took
a second to thank them.

Then he got back to barking as the patient's heart rate suddenly dropped down to
thirty and he commenced cardiac massage.
'He needs intubating,' he told Lina, as if she
were a schoolgirl on work experience. 'Can
you take over the massage while I—?'

'Fine,' Lina said, not remotely fazed that
it was just the two of them. After all, that
was how she usually worked.

The drugs were already pulled up and
the intubation kit opened, so that even as
he spoke she was taking over the massage
while he quickly got some drugs into the
unfortunate man and then looked around
for another IVAC pump.

'There's one there.' Lina nodded as she
pumped on the man's chest.

It was all very quickly done, and very
soon Mr James was intubated and with the

drugs circulating in his system thankfully soon had a decent cardiac output. In fact, by the time the anaesthetist and cardiologist had arrived his blood pressure was improving.

'How are we doing?' May popped her head around the curtain.

'All good.' Garth nodded. 'We're going to move him up to the catheter suite. How's the young girl?'

'They're moving her up to ICU. Garth, can you speak to her relatives again? They really don't understand just how critical she is.'

'Sure.' He nodded.

'What about this one?' May asked. 'Any relatives?'

'No. There's just an ex-wife so far,' Lina responded, going through his wallet. 'There's nothing on his phone.'

'Well, why don't I take over here,' May suggested, 'while you try and find out some more?'

As she stepped out, Dianne was preparing the overdose patient for her move to ICU. Lina was more than used to working backwards to glean details and so she headed to Reception and Triage and did her best to piece together events, but she returned to Section A a short while later really none the wiser.

Lina found Garth as he came out from speaking with the OD's family and told him the little she had been able to glean. 'The only contact I can find is an ex-wife. I've tried to call his work but given that it's midnight I haven't had much luck…'

'No ICE contact on his phone.'

'No,' Lina said, because she had checked what she could access and unfortunately there were no details. 'I'm waiting for someone from the hotel to call me back, though they weren't exactly helpful.'

'Well, I'd better call the ex-wife,' Garth said. 'I wonder how pleased she'll be to hear from me, though…'

'She'll probably appreciate knowing, but even if not she might be able to point you in the right direction…' She paused. He was a consultant after all and would know all this, but it didn't stop her adding, 'They might have children together.' She gave a pale smile. This patient really was a little close to the bone for her—not that Garth could know that. Her own father had suffered a major heart attack years ago and they hadn't found out until thirty-six hours later.

She didn't want the same for the family of Mr James.

'Well, I'll go and call her. Thank you,' he added. 'Good job.'

'And you,' Lina said, just as she would if it were Brendan, or any other colleague. 'Well done.' She saw May approaching and gave her a smile. 'I'm just heading back to Section B.'

'No, I'm closing it,' May said. 'You go and take first break.' Lina's lips pressed together a fraction—first break was the one no one wanted because it made the rest of the night a very long one.

May must have seen the press of her lips. 'If you don't want first break then come and work for us full time and you'll get your pick of dinner breaks.'

'I'm not that desperate.' Lina smiled and headed to the kitchenette where she made a coffee and took her lunchbox from the fridge. She then made her way to the staffroom, and long before she was hungry opened up the foil on her tuna, lettuce and mayo sandwiches.

'Gawd.' Les, the porter, waved his hands in the air. 'You don't change, do you? If it's not eggs you're eating it's tuna.'

'I need the protein to keep me going.' Lina laughed. 'Do you want one?'

'Might as well if I've got to sit here and smell it,' Les harrumphed, taking one of the offered sandwiches. 'They've had me running up to ICU twice. Running at my age…'

'I can't run,' Lina admitted.

'Well, jogging,' Les conceded.

'I can't jog either. A brisk walk, maybe…' They laughed and they chatted and moaned, but not for long—Les was soon buzzed to take another patient to the ward. Sitting there alone, her sandwiches done, Lina was too full to contemplate the Welsh cake and, ten minutes before her break ended, decided to head back out to the unit. Before she made it to Section A, though, she saw Brendan, making up a stretcher, having just brought a patient in.

'Hey.' Lina smiled, and given she wasn't yet due back from her break she stopped for a little chat. 'How's it been?'

'Busy,' Brendan said, and told her about a stabbing that had brought them over this way, and then the patient they had just brought in—Mrs Amy Hill. 'She's confused. Just lost her husband over Christmas and keeps asking where he is, poor lady. She was fine yesterday, according to her carer—as bright as a button.' She liked it that Brendan really took the time and care to find out about his patients.

'How are things your end?' Brendan asked as he threw the blankets into the linen skip and then did a double take when he looked up. 'What happened to your eyebrows?'

'Shona tinted them,' Lina said. 'I feel like Groucho Marx '

'Who?' Brendan frowned and then got back to finding out about her night. 'What's it like on the other side?'

'Good!' Lina replied enthusiastically. 'We had a STEMI.' Odd to some, but Brendan gave an appreciative nod as she told him how well it had gone, but she could see his mind was wandering and as he took out his phone to check it, she guessed where his thoughts had gone. 'How's Alison?'

'We were in here earlier. Alison thought she'd gone into labour and we spent the afternoon up on Maternity,' Brendan said worriedly. 'They put her on the monitor for a couple of hours and then sent her home. The midwife said she didn't think it would be too long. I just hate leaving her on her own...'

'I know you do.' Lina put a sympathetic hand on his arm. Brendan was, she was certain, going to faint when his beloved Alison actually went into labour and she repeated the same platitudes that she had, over and over, in recent weeks. 'I honestly think if something was happening, Alison would let you know straight away.'

'Really?'

'Yes,' Lina said patiently. 'She'd be straight on the phone to you.'

'I know you're right, it's just…'

'You're worried.'

'I'm beside myself,' Brendan admitted. 'And bloody Peter…' He nodded at his partner for the night. 'He's told me to stop banging on. Said he's sick of hearing about it. I tell you this much, I miss you tonight, Lina…'

'I know.' Peter maybe did have a point, Lina thought, but Brendan was just, well, Brendan, and currently, in the moments between patients, the only thing on his mind was Alison and their baby. 'Just ignore him,' Lina said. 'Maybe you could—'

But she never got to finish as her name was being abruptly called by Garth.

'Lina!' There was a bark of command in his voice as he walked towards them. 'When the two of you have finished your little get-together, could I ask you to sort out cubicle five so we can get the patient off the corridor?'

'Sure,' Lina said. 'We were just finishing up anyway.' Not that he was waiting to hear it. Garth was already striding off and she rolled her eyes at Brendan. 'He's not the friendliest, apparently,' she said. 'I'd better go.'

'And he'd better watch it.' Brendan smiled. 'That poor guy clearly has no idea who he's dealing with!'

Garth didn't—Lina was not one to be told off for no reason and stay silent. Working out on the road, she'd long ago learned to be assertive, even if she found it difficult at times. Though it still didn't come naturally to her, she had found it far better to stand up for herself at the start of rumblings than to simply let things slide.

And, for whatever reason, Garth was starting to rumble!

Cubicle five was a mess, but soon it was clean and restocked and ready for the next patient. Lina, though, was cross and when Garth stuck his head in to make sure the cubicle had been prepared, she put in her request: 'Can I have a quick word, please?'

'Of course,' he said, and stepped into the cubicle and gave her his attention.

'I was actually on my break back there when you told me off in the middle of the corridor...' Lina said. 'I don't need to be spoken to as if I've been caught talking in class, when the fact is...'

She stopped, not because she had run out of words, more because she had run out of breath, for it held in her lungs. His dark eyes were as navy as the blue hour, and now that she properly met them, she found they were just as captivating. She caught the very male scent of him, like soapy rain with a hint of citrus that was both subtle and lingering. And for someone who had sworn off men, she was fast finding it wasn't quite that simple.

It was physical, Lina told herself, remembering that she was angry, and with the little breath she could summon she spoke on. 'I have every right to talk to someone, without being told off—'

'You do, and I apologise.' Not satisfied with stealing her breath, he now took the wind from her sails as he spoke on. 'I was completely out of line.'

'Oh!' She hadn't been expecting that. Lina had thought there would be if not a disagreement, then at least a little snap back from him, or some lecture, but instead he had straight away admitted to being in the wrong.

'Apology accepted,' Lina said.

'Thank you.'

'I'll go and bring in the patient.' As Lina walked off, she found that she was holding her breath and that her cheeks felt warm, as if there had been words…yet there hadn't been.

His apology had been unexpected and she felt all churned up, but not in an angry way.

It was all very polite, and also a little disquieting, in a way she couldn't properly define.

A slight rumbling of her own, perhaps.

CHAPTER TWO

'MRS HILL?' LINA checked the name band and notes and saw that it was the patient Brendan had brought in. Her observations were of concern, as was her blood glucose, which was rather high. She was restless and sweaty and needed to be seen. 'I'm going to bring you through now.'

Mrs Hill was tiny and feisty and over eighty—and very much did not want to be in the emergency department on a Friday night. 'I want to go home,' she kept saying as Lina got her undressed and did a set of obs.

'Well, hopefully you soon shall be,' Lina said, 'but first we need the doctor to take a look.' Only Huba was in the suture theatre with a patient who looked as if he might take a while. 'She really does need to be seen,' Lina explained, a little unsure as to why Huba was suturing when Dianne was assigned to be in here. 'She's febrile and very dehydrated…'

'Could you ask someone else?' she said, and held up her gloved hands. 'I've only just started.'

'Sure,' Lina responded, and as she came out of Theatre she saw May's slight raised eyebrow.

'Is Huba still in there?' May gave a shake of her head. 'Desmond should have finished an hour ago but is still tied up. I think Garth is just finishing up with a patient in Resus.'

'Okay.'

Garth was indeed just finishing up, but clearly had plenty else to be getting on with. 'Where's Huba?'

'Suturing,' Lina said, and watched his dark eyes glance down the packed corridor and the lines of paramedics waiting for their patients to even be assessed. He let out a tense breath and then took the admission card, but still he gave a very nice smile when he introduced himself to the patient. 'How are you, Mrs Hill?'

'Isn't it your job to tell me?' she asked. 'There's no reason for me to be here, I just want to go home.'

'Where is home?' Garth asked, as if politely making conversation while he read through the doctor's letter.

'You know full well where it is,' Mrs Hill retorted. 'It's written on the paper you're holding.'

'Okay,' Garth said, and he was very kind and patient with her as he went through a few other details and checked with her the medications she was on.

'It's all in the letter.'

'Okay,' he said. 'I'm just going to examine you, if that's okay.'

'No,' she said, her voice rising. 'It is not okay. I just want to go home.'

'Where are you, Mrs Hill?'

'Hospital.'

He questioned her very gently and Lina watched as the old lady battled to answer him, deflecting his questions at every turn.

'What does it matter!' she shouted when he asked her the year. 'With the mess the world's in.'

'I think you're confused, Mrs Hill,' he said. 'And trying very hard not to show it.'

'Wouldn't you be?' She sank back on the pillows and tears filled her hazel eyes. 'I don't know what's going on. There were men in my bedroom. They took me out of my bed.'

'That was the paramedics,' Lina said, and took the lady's hand. 'I know it must have given you a dreadful fright, but the district nurse was worried about you when she came to give you your medication for the night and I believe the GP called for an ambulance.'

'How did they get in?' She turned anxious eyes towards Lina.

'Your carer gave them the code.' Lina had seen it so many times, and she took a moment to explain things to the lady who had had such a terrible scare. 'Apparently you weren't yourself.' She looked over at Garth. 'Mrs Hill's just lost her husband.'

'Now, that wasn't in the note,' Garth said. 'I'm very sorry to hear that, Mrs Hill. When did your husband die?'

'It was my first Christmas without him.'

Finally they were getting somewhere.

'You're very dehydrated,' Garth said, checking the skin turgor on her hands.

'Bert used to bring me my tea.'

'It's hard,' he said, 'when those routines change, but we need to replace those fluids and I need to find out what's wrong with you.'

'I miss him.'

'Of course you do,' Garth said. 'What would Bert say if he were here?'

She gave a grudging smile. 'To let the doctor do his job.'

'Then will you let me do that please?'

She did, and Lina liked how he took his time with Mrs Hill, explained things carefully to her, and seemed to understand her proud struggle to hold onto normality. 'Your blood sugar is a little high, as is your temperature…' Now that she let him, he examined her carefully then took some blood and commenced an IV and asked Lina to obtain a urine specimen.

'I hate this,' Mrs Hill said as Lina sorted out the specimen.

'I'm sure you do,' Lina agreed, and listened as Amy reminisced about Bert. 'He never missed my morning tea,' she said, as she told her about all the little things her late husband had done for her. 'I tend to forget, but he never did.'

She seemed a lot more settled by the time Lina left her—with the curtains wide open and in full view of the nurses' station.

'How is she now?' Garth asked as Lina sent off the specimens.

'Settling,' Lina said, and she gave him a smile. Then her choice of word wavered because he nodded, but instead of getting back to his notes there was a brief suspension of time, which was, well, unsettling.

Nicely so.

Just a nod from him and a smile from her, except the small non-event took too long in her mind and when he didn't immediately turn and resume his notes...well, it seemed to take too long for Garth also.

'That's good,' he said.

'Yes.'

'I suspect a UTI. She's probably been neglecting herself a bit.'

'Yes, I think Bert took care of that side of things.' She paused. 'Well, he brought her tea and checked her blood glucose...'

'I'll wait for all the results,' Garth said, 'but she needs a geriatric referral. I'm sure the UTI is exacerbating things but there may be some underlying confusion that Bert was handling.'

Lina nodded. 'Or she's just grieving.'

'Yes.'

It was a completely normal conversation, except it felt different to Lina. He opened his mouth as if to say something, but then clearly decided otherwise and he climbed down from his stool and spoke to May. 'Is Huba still in Theatre?'

'Yes.'

He headed off in the direction of the theatres and Lina stood, a bit *unsettled* still.

'You okay, Lina?' May checked.

Apart from a sudden crush on your grumpy consultant? Lina thought. 'Fine,' she replied.

It was all very disquieting, this odd feeling of hers, this awareness of *them*. At around four in the morning, when the department was slowing down and he was updating charts on the computer and May took the chance for a little catch-up, she *felt* him listening.

'Is it nice to be back?' May asked her.

'It is,' Lina agreed. 'I always enjoy my shifts here.'

'I'm sure we could find a spot on the roster for you. If you ever do decide to come back to nursing you're to be sure and let me know.'

'Come back to nursing?' Garth glanced over.

So he *had* been listening, Lina thought. 'Lina's switched and is now a paramedic,' said May. 'She did all her nursing placements here but still comes back to us now and then…'

'Oh,' Garth said, and their eyes met, just for a second but long enough to know he was perhaps replaying the conversation he'd overheard between her and Brendan. Lina gave the tiniest triumphant smile, because he *really* had had no right to tell her off.

'Wasn't that your partner in earlier?' May asked. 'Brendan. I thought I saw him.'

Lina nodded. 'He's on with Peter tonight.'

'God help him, then.' May smiled. 'Brendan's baby must be due any day now?'

'No, another three weeks or so,' Lina corrected, 'though Brendan's quite sure it will be tonight. Mind you, he's been saying that for days. Alison's booked to have the baby here, so I'm sure you'll all know.'

'He'll be passing around the cigars.' May smiled again. 'He's so excited.'

Lina didn't carry on the conversation. She was having trouble focussing on it, and that was rare for her, but she felt impatient almost for a pause just to think.

She was all churned up and unsure quite why.

'You're quiet, Lina,' May commented, as she filled out tomorrow's on-call board in preparation for the day staff.

'Am I?'

Perhaps she was, but she was just so conscious of Garth. It was ridiculous really, because he was completely out of her league—and that *wasn't* her being self-effacing.

Garth Hughes was stunning looking, and if her foray into online dating had taught Lina anything it was that she was fair to middling at best.

'Did that STEMI upset you?' May checked, briefly glancing over her shoulder.

'No,' Lina said, 'that's what we live for…' It sounded a bit flippant, but as paramedics it was a condition they were well trained to face. But then her dark humour could no longer deflect, because in truth it had upset her. Maybe that was why she was all churned up. 'Maybe a bit,' she admitted. 'I mean, following up and trying to find the family and things, it just, well…'

'It reminds you of your dad?'

Lina glanced up. Of course May knew that her father had had a near fatal heart attack years ago while overseas. Well, May knew the gist, though Lina had never revealed to anyone the circumstances that had surrounded it.

May was right—the STEMI *had* unsettled her.

'Yes,' Lina admitted. 'It did upset me a bit.'

Garth found that he was waiting for Lina to elaborate.

She did not.

And he found he was grateful for May's nosy nature, and wished for her to persevere with her line of questioning.

Yet she did not.

Instead, May asked a work question. 'Are you on tonight, Garth?'

'No,' Garth said. He was about to return to his notes but, reminding himself that he was supposed to be trying harder to be more sociable, added, 'I'll be unpacking.'

'Unpacking?' May said, clearly so surprised at this snippet of freely given information that she turned around.

'I moved into a flat on my break...'

'Oh!'

'It's very bare,' Garth elaborated, 'and now that all their furniture is out of the place, I'm starting to see that I might have bought a whole lot of trouble for myself.'

'So you've bought?'

'Yes.'

'Where?'

'Close by,' he responded crisply. Lina could almost feel his reluctance as he answered May's question. 'It's not within walking distance, though,' he added. 'Or you'd be forever dropping in with something for me to sign...'

'I would too,' May said. 'Well, I guess if you've bought then you can't just up and run away.' May smiled, though her eyes met his and Garth knew she had seen his résumé and the multiple work locations over the last six years or so. Scotland, the Midlands, the south. Prior to that it had all been Wales. And, yes, the fact that he had bought a property for the first time in the said six years possibly spoke volumes. But for once May didn't delve further, just gave him a small smile and got back to updating the board. 'Looks like we're keeping you, then!'

'Looks that way. Right.' He stood up and yawned. 'I'm going to have something to eat, but call if you need me. Where's Huba?'

'Hiding in Theatre,' May said.

'Hiding?' Lina checked once Garth was gone.

'She's lost her confidence.' May nodded. 'You were working on the night of the house fire, weren't you?'

'Yes.' Lina nodded. 'I brought the mother in.'

'Well, poor Huba's taking some fallout from it and between you and me it's knocked her for six. Garth is doing his best to help her regain her confidence, but she second-guesses everything, or else she hides. Why do you think I closed Section B? Huba would still be down there now if she had her way.'

Ahh, now things were making a little more sense, and Lina conceded to herself that she had read the interaction between Garth and Huba wrong—he hadn't been reluctant to come down, it had been Huba berating herself for having to ask him.

'Goodness,' Lina sighed. 'Poor thing.'

'She'll get there,' May said assuredly. 'It's good she's got Garth looking out for her. For all I moan about his social skills, there's no one better to have in your corner.'

'Social skills?' Lina checked. 'He seems fine.'

'Sure enough, he's chatty tonight. Perhaps the break did him some good after all.'

With Garth gone and Huba hiding, everyone was busy, so Lina had a couple of minutes while she was restocking to hold a rather tricky conversation. 'May,' Lina ventured, 'I've got something I need to ask you.'

'You *do* want to come and work full time!'

'No.' Lina gave a tense smile. 'I've applied for a job and I wondered if I could put you down as a preliminary reference. I haven't told work yet…' Her lips pulled to the side as May turned around. 'I haven't told anyone.'

'Where's this job.'

'Newcastle,' Lina said.

'That's a long way off.'

'I know, and that's why I haven't said anything to anyone yet.'

'But your family's here in London, you've got friends in London...'

'Yes, but I can't afford a place of my own!' Lina said. 'I'm so over sharing. Dad was born in Newcastle and I've got some family there. I love it... We used to holiday there all the time.'

'But your life is here, Lina.'

'And I can make a new one there...' She went quiet as Huba came in. 'Hey.' Lina smiled.

'Where's Garth?'

'On his break,' May said, and then glanced over at Lina and gave a nod to their earlier conversation about May being a referee.

'Of course...' She nodded, but looked a touch confused rather than pleased.

Lina felt rather the same, but there was little time to dwell because patients were still coming in, and the results from Mrs Hill had also come through. Her potassium was raised so Lina ran them past Huba.

'How is she now?' Huba asked.

'Sound asleep,' Lina said, 'and I think the

fluids have helped as she's a little more ori-
entated.

'Would you bring her over to Resus?'
Huba said. 'With a potassium that high she
should be monitored.'

'Sure.'

'And maybe I should call Garth back,'
Huba added.

'Lina was just going to get him to sign for
a patient,' May interjected. 'She can let him
know the results.'

Having put Mrs Hill on a monitor, Lina
headed to the staffroom. She found that
Garth was dozing with his head back on the
chair, his eyes closed and his mouth slightly
open. There was a feeling of recognition that
stilled Lina and she stood there, confused
for a second, and not quite knowing why.

Oh, that's right, she was to tell him about
Mrs Hill.

Only it wasn't that.

Lina had the oddest feeling that she knew
him, that she'd seen him before.

Well, of course she had, she told herself.
He'd probably been on when she'd brought
in patients... except it felt like something
more.

Garth must have felt her standing there

staring at him, for his eyes opened then and he turned his head and gave her a look.

'Is everything okay?'

'Of course,' Lina said, blushing at being caught looking, so to speak, and still she couldn't shake the feeling that she knew him from somewhere. 'I just need your signature on a couple of things and Mrs Hill's labs are starting to come back.' She ran through the more pressing ones.

'Okay.'

'May's just putting her on a monitor.'

'I'll come around.'

'Sure.'

'You're okay?' he checked.

'Of course,' Lina said, realising she was acting a bit oddly, though he clearly assumed it was for a different reason.

'I would never have known that the STEMI upset you until May said so. You were very efficient back there.'

'Thank you.'

'And if your father...' He gave a grim smile. 'Well, I'm very sorry.'

'My dad's not dead,' Lina said.

'Glad to hear it.'

'He travelled for work a lot and had a heart attack in a hotel in Singapore...'

'Ahh. Now I see…'

Only he didn't see. In fact, not even May, not even Brendan, knew the full story, but she found herself telling him. 'It was how my mum found out that he was having an affair.'

'Oh.'

'Yes. "Oh!"' Lina nodded. 'Well, that wasn't my mother's response, exactly.'

'How did she find out?'

'She didn't,' Lina said. 'Well, not for thirty-six hours. Everyone assumed his girlfriend was his next of kin…' She met his eyes. 'How did Mr James's ex-wife take it?'

'She's on her way now,' Garth said. 'She's probably already here. You were right, they do have children together.'

'Well, it's good that they all know.' She went to turn.

'I'm sorry,' he said, but in a different tone from the one he'd used before. 'It can't have been a great way to find out.'

'No,' Lina admitted.

'Did your mum go?' He was curious, in spite of telling himself to hold back. It was just that she intrigued him so. 'To Singapore, when she heard?'

'No,' Lina said. 'She went to visit a lawyer instead. Odd, isn't it…?'

'Odd?'

'I think I'd have jumped on the plane if only to slap him for being such an idiot to cheat on me… Well, not me, but you know what I mean…'

'I know what you mean.' He almost smiled, just a whisper of one, but Lina found herself wishing that his gorgeous, full mouth might stretch into one.

Oh!

And so rather than stand there wishing and thinking such things, she gabbled on quickly. 'I think we can all count ourselves lucky there was just an ex-wife in the picture tonight.'

She headed back to the unit, where they did their best to get the department in shape for the morning staff and clear the decks as much as was possible.

'And they'll still moan that we didn't wipe the trolleys down or something,' May muttered. 'Thank God I'm back on days next week.'

Her last job for the night was taking Mrs Hill up to the geriatric unit, and though the patient had dreaded it, she was greeted very warmly and soon settled into a bed with a huge warm cover.

'Breakfast is coming round shortly,' the

accepting nurse told Mrs Hill, 'but I'll see if I can find you a cup of tea to settle you in.'

'They'll look after you here,' Lina said, glad to see Mrs Hill looking so much more relaxed and knowing that she was in the right place.

By the time she was back on the ward, May was getting ready to start handover. 'Once you've made up the trolley, you can get off,' she said as she signed Lina's time sheet. 'Thanks, Lina, it's been lovely to have you with us…' Her voice faded and then she excused herself from the handover for a moment and pulled Lina aside in a way only May could. 'Call me,' she said. 'If you want to chat.'

Lina was touched that May would actually stop the handover just to reach out to her. 'Thanks, May.'

'And of course I'll give you a reference, but don't go jumping into anything. Talk it through with me, if you like…'

She might just do that, Lina thought as she had a quick freshen up at the sink in the changing rooms. Throwing her scrubs into the linen bin, Lina managed a wry smile as she caught her reflection in the rather speckled long mirror.

Her gorgeous satin amber underwear, her

only fashion weakness, would of course go unnoticed, but it always cheered her up anyway.

And that little dash of feminine luxury made her feel, well, better, that was all, even as she pulled on dark jeans and a huge grey jumper and then zipped on her boots. To that she added a large coat and very long scarf and headed out.

'See you, Lina!' Dianne called as she took the shortcut through the department to the exit. 'Nice working with you.'

'And you.' Lina smiled. 'See you.'

'Not too soon, I hope...' May teased, and Lina laughed, understanding that May was referring to the fact that she generally arrived in the department as a paramedic with a stretcher containing a patient.

'Thanks for the sandwich,' Les added, as he dragged a couple of oxygen cylinders for exchange. 'Though put less salt on them next time.'

They were a mad lot and Lina's smile remained unseen as she walked out of the department.

Except her smile was not quite unseen.

Garth Hughes glanced up from a patient's relative he was speaking to as a certain Lina Edwards left the department. His head told him to just let her leave, except he couldn't fully listen to logic right now. 'Excuse me a moment,' he said politely to the relative. 'Lina...' he called.

He watched as she turned, a slight flush to her cheeks, and he looked into vivid green eyes. It had been a long time since he had found himself intrigued by a woman. Aside from attraction, Garth couldn't quite pin-point what it was that enthralled him, just that if he didn't do something now, he had no idea when or if he might see her again, and that suddenly mattered an awful lot. 'Could I have a quick word before you go?'

'Is there another cubicle you want me to clean?' she teased, and he smiled a wry smile that felt like *such* a reward for a night's work.

For his smile did not come easily, that much Lina had gleaned.

'About that—' he started, but Lina cut in.

'Really, it's fine.'

'Actually, it isn't,' Garth said. 'It would seem that I owe you a double apology.'

'Double?' Lina checked.

'Yes. Do you want to get breakfast once I'm done, so I can better apologise?'

'Breakfast?' Lina frowned as he nodded.

'Yes, and not at the canteen. I'd rather take

this conversation away from May's exceptionally beady eyes. There's a café next to the hospital where we could meet.'

'There's a better one around the corner,' Lina said and told him the name. 'One of the perks of my job is knowing where to get breakfast.'

'I'll see you there then,' Garth said. 'Just as soon as I can get away.'

'Sure.'

'I might be a while—it depends what time Richard gets in and how busy we are.'

'It's fine,' Lina said. 'I'm very used to shifts going over.'

'Thanks.'

What she wasn't used to was sexy consultants asking to meet her for a private conversation. It was unexpected and it was unsettlingly nice.

Or, rather, Garth was unexpected and unsettlingly nice.

CHAPTER THREE

'LINA!'

She was known at the café too, although out of her paramedic uniform perhaps not quite so recognisable.

'I didn't realise it was you. The usual?'

Her usual here was a coffee and almond croissant but, though her stomach was pleading for carbs as it always did after a night shift, she decided to wait for Garth and shook her head. 'Just a coffee, thanks, and I'll have it here.'

'Sure.' The barista smiled and then asked the question that was on everyone's lips, because Alison and Brendan lived nearby: 'Has Brendan had his baby yet?'

'Not yet.' Lina smiled back and rolled her eyes. 'I'm sure we'll all know the very second it happens.'

The café was half-empty and she chose a seat by the window and then peered into her bag and looked for something, anything that might freshen up her appearance a touch, despite knowing it was pointless. Unlike Shona, who carried a kit that could transmute her from bedraggled to ravishing in seconds, Lina carried a plastic zip lock bag, the contents of which she'd already used— just a toothbrush and toothpaste, some deodorant and such. There wasn't even a lip balm hiding inside.

So instead of tarting herself up for her unexpected breakfast date, she gazed out of the window, telling herself it wasn't a date…

Yet she had a feeling that Garth didn't often ask the casual nurse out at the end of her shift.

Or, knowing her luck with men, maybe he did; perhaps that was his modus operandi…

But it would be a while before she found out. Lina was at the end of her second coffee when he arrived, dressed in a heavy grey coat, which he hung on the hook. He had changed into black jeans and a jumper but even casually dressed there was a certain elegance to him.

And sexiness.

She'd been trying to ignore that fact all night, but now, outside work and about to sit face to face with him, it was as if her body finally allowed itself to acknowledge it, and she surprised herself by blushing.

Her blush was, she guessed, as rare as his smile.

'Hey,' he said, and took a seat. 'Sorry I took so long.'

'It's not a problem. I was going to get something to eat before I headed home. It's quite a way…'

'Where is home?'

He raised his eyebrows when she told him it was the other side of London. 'But I lived here when I did my nursing.'

'Have you eaten then?'

'No.'

She ordered her usual almond croissant and, deciding a third coffee might be a bit much if she was to have any hope of sleeping, chose tea. Garth chose the same, as well as a toasted sandwich.

'You were a nurse before you did paramedicine?'

'Well, a student.' Lina nodded. 'I didn't enjoy it as much as I'd expected to, though. I thought I'd made the wrong choice until I did my Accident and Emergency placement, except…' Her voice trailed off, guessing he didn't really want to know.

'What?'

'I found that I was jealous of the para-medics.'

'Really?'

She nodded. 'I found myself wanting to know what had happened before the patient arrived. May was brilliant; she arranged a couple of ride-alongs for me...' Their food arrived and there was a pause in the conversation as they both eyed their excellent choices.

'This looks so good,' Garth said, examining his sandwich.

'They know what shift staff need,' Lina agreed. 'These croissants are delivered at six each morning...' She tore her own open as she resumed their conversation. 'Anyway, I finished my nursing but then went on to study paramedicine and now here I am...' she looked up into those navy eyes '...sitting in a café on a Saturday morning waiting to find out why I'm owed a double apology.'

'I had no right to tell you off when you were on your break. Correction: I had no right to tell you off when I did.'

'We've already covered that.'

'I assumed that he was your partner, or boyfriend, or something along those lines...'

'God, no.' Lina pulled a face. 'What on earth gave you that idea?'

'When he said he was missing you.'

Lina smiled. 'He's missing me because I'm good to work with.'

'You are.'

'Can't have the staff flirting at work,' Lina teased, and then paused as she realised it was now she who had perhaps misunderstood.

'It irked me,' Garth said.

Her lips began to round to form the W in 'why' and she suddenly wished she'd bothered with that lip balm as his gorgeous gaze fell down to there and realisation struck... and her *why* changed to a surprised 'oh!'

But she was still doubting her own conclusions. Was Garth saying that he liked her or was she jumping ahead?

'It irked me a lot,' Garth said, and then clarified, 'I don't get involved with people at work—deliberately so. I was just wondering if I should make an exception to my own rule when I saw you talking to your partner, who, as it turns out, isn't a partner in that sense... I came over high-handed. I'm not exactly Mr Sociable, but I don't go hauling out the staff for talking. At least, not normally...'

'It's fine.' Lina smiled, and actually it was better than fine. It really was the nicest apol-

ogy she had ever received. His honesty was
refreshing and his complete lack of game-
playing as he told her that he liked her meant
she felt able to admit to the same: 'I'm glad
it irked you.'

'I'm glad that you're glad. I've worked at
The Primary for six months now and our
paths have never crossed. I'm sure I'd remember if they had...'

'I think they did,' Lina said, because she
was sure now that she recognised him, but
rather unsure how she could forget such a
delicious detail. 'We're often there—well,
not often, but...' She tried to place him and
then suddenly she thought she had it. 'Were
you working the night of the house fire?
Huba said you were...'

'Yes and no,' Garth said. 'I was called in,
but...' He cast his mind back. 'I think all
the patients had been admitted by the time
I got there. I'm certain I'd remember you.'

She nodded because she had thought exactly the same.

'What I'm trying to say is that I don't
want to wait possibly another six months
until our paths cross again.'

'I'm there all the time.'

They ate and they chatted, and while
some of it was about work she mentioned

her upcoming break, though there was a detail she left out: he certainly didn't need to know about her possible relocation to Newcastle… 'I'm wandering,' Lina said. 'Well, walking, I suppose.'

'Rambling?' he asked.

'No, walking.' Lina smiled. 'I go from one bed and breakfast to the next…'

'Trekking?'

'Walking.' Lina laughed. 'And while I do I come across plenty of trekkers and ramblers and such, but I really am not in that category. In my case there are also a lot of shops involved…' She opened her mouth to tell him about the antique shops and her obsession with vintage toy ambulances and such, but remembering Brendan's words decided instead to hold back a touch. 'I walk with a backpack and sometimes I take a bus or train, and in the evening I go to a bar or a nice restaurant or grab a takeaway. I have a map of the UK and Ireland on my wall and I tick off every town and village I've visited, all the ones where I've had a coffee or meal or glass of wine. Just passing through doesn't count.'

'How much have you covered.?'

'Not nearly enough, but I'm making a dent. I just plan my route and walk and…'

'What?'

'Breathe,' Lina said, 'and think, or don't think...'

'Sounds wonderful.'

She nodded. 'It is. Work's brilliant for it. I'm cramming my next lot of shifts and then heading to the Scottish borders in a couple of weeks.'

'Are you driving up?'

'No, I don't have a car. Anyway, I'll sleep on the train and that gives me four full days of just me and a rucksack.'

'You travel light.'

'Not when you're carrying it. It's just nice to get away, to see the country...' She took a breath. 'To put things into perspective, though...' She stopped.

Slow down, she told herself, because she found herself opening up far too easily where Garth Hughes was concerned.

Find his fault.

Find the reason he's...

She tried to gauge his age and put him in his mid-thirties and, given the flirting, hopefully single.

They hadn't got onto all that. It was just so much fun getting to know each other, except now it was late. Well, it was morning

for some, but by night duty standards it was late—late and out of the blue. Lina yawned.

'Am I boring you?' he teased.

It was honestly tempting to switch her seat just to sit next to him, but instead, while the going was so good, it really was time for her to go to bed. 'You know you're not.' Lina smiled and stared back into those navy eyes that looked deep into hers. He tripped the switch in her heart and made flirting, at which she was usually terrible, so simple. 'I just need to go to bed.'

Another mutual smile but, gosh, it would be far too soon when they hadn't as much as kissed, yet... She was going crazy, Lina decided. Too little sleep did poor decisions make, and so she made her excuses and nipped to the loo.

'Go home!' she said to her reflection in the mirror and, as she walked out, she signalled to pay the bill, except the barista told her that it had been taken care of.

She walked over to Garth. 'Thanks,' she said.

'No problem.'

They walked out into rain and sunshine combined, the type of day where you had to squint at the brightness just before the sun dipped behind an angry cloud, and the rain

felt cold. It felt so right to give in and face each other.

'You spoiled my line,' Lina said. And then he pulled her towards him and they kissed, something they had both secretly wanted for hours now.

Hours!

Oh, how they kissed.

He put his hands on either side of her face and his touch was so warm and tender. Their tongues mingled and it was like being drawn down a tunnel, into a vortex of delicious want. The sound of traffic seemed to dull and the cold disappeared and the rain felt delicious on their skin. His hands moved down so that they rested on her hips and they kissed slowly and languidly but with a deepening passion.

Nine a. m. kisses on a cold winter morning were surprisingly dangerous.

His eyes really were the darkest yet also the brightest blue, and they were staring deep into her own. There was a slight breathlessness between them, a gorgeous feeling of excitement, as if they were standing on the very edge of a mountain, surveying the view together.

'What *was* your line?' Garth asked.

'When you thanked me for paying I would have said, "You can get the next one…"'

'Ah.' Garth smiled. 'Well, I *am* getting the next one, and hopefully it will be tonight…'

Shona would no doubt tell her she should have said, *No, I can't tonight*, and not appear too keen and free on a Saturday, but feeling his body all warm and toned and pressed against her, it was impossible for Lina to feign nonchalance. 'Yes please…' Between kisses they sorted out the details. 'I really do have to go,' Lina said, 'or I'll be falling asleep on the tube and end up—'

'No,' Garth said, 'I'll drive you home.'

'Don't be daft.'

'Lina, I've kept you waiting an hour after your shift. It's the least I can do.'

Goodness!

Now, this was something she wasn't used to.

Lina's shifts often ended hours after their intended time and she was very used to just accepting the tired ride home, battling not to fall asleep and miss her stop.

It was incredibly nice to be spoiled with a lift.

They walked to his apartment, which actually was just around the corner from the hospital. 'Don't tell May how close it is,' he said, and thankfully he was sensible enough not to suggest that she come up.

Instead, they went to the underground car park and soon Lina was in his lovely warm car and being driven home. It was perfect—well, apart from his terrible taste in music, but Lina felt it was rather too early for her to say so.

But then…

'What *is* this?' she suddenly asked.

'Great, isn't it?' he said, misreading her question as enthusiasm. He glanced over and named some band she'd never heard of. Lina blinked, because it was like having root-canal treatment, but she chose to keep quiet—after all, he'd been so nice to give her a lift home.

And when they arrived at her flat, he kissed her so nicely and slowly goodbye that the boopy-doop music even slowed tempo and curled round her mind.

Bed!

With him!

She wanted to wilt and give in to temptation and invite him in, but she didn't want to endure the rise of Shona's eyebrows if she brought a guy home from work.

They both stared at each other for the longest time, as if a missing person had just been safely returned.

'I'm going up,' Lina said. She looked at the smudges under his eyes and knew he had quite a drive home. 'You'll be okay to drive?'

'I will be,' Garth said, 'but it's tempting to say I might need a lie down first…'

They were both laughing, and kissing, but Lina said again, 'I'm going up,' and this time prised herself off him.

She floated up the stairs and into her tiny flat, then ran to the living room window, and there he was, looking up. She felt like Rapunzel and wanted to let down her hair, certain that if she did he would climb up.

'Uh-oh.' Shona came in from the kitchen, holding a huge mug of coffee. 'I've seen that look before.'

'No, you haven't,' Lina said, because she had actually never felt like this before. 'He gave me a lift home.'

'Really?'

'He's nice—well, except for his taste in music…'

'So when are you seeing him again?'

'Tonight.' Lina beamed, and Shona did the same. With her flatmate going out, it meant that she had the place to herself.

Or rather to herself and her boyfriend, Marcus.

Lina was positive, *positive* that Shona was about to ask if he could move in. He practically lived here already.

That was the trouble with flat sharing, as Lina had long since found out…

Anyway, she was too tired to think about that now so she had a quick shower and then made a mug of tea to take to bed. As she waited for the kettle to boil, she went to rinse out her lunchbox. But there, nestled inside, wrapped in tissue, was the Welsh cake she had taken last night and forgotten about.

''Night,' she said to Shona, even though it was the middle of the morning.

'Do you want to be woken up?'

'About five if you're around,' Lina said. 'Thanks.'

One of the absolute perks of night shift was closing the curtains on a wet, rainy day and climbing into bed with a huge mug of tea.

And a Welsh cake.

They might, as Garth had said, have tasted better on the day they had been made, but the sweet and spicy buttery biscuit was delicious, possibly more so because it had come from him.

Garth Hughes.

She had a date on a Saturday night, like a normal person, and not with someone who wouldn't match their photo, or who would be disappointed when they actually saw her in the flesh.

Or would he be?

Lina fell asleep thinking about her rather bland wardrobe and utter lack of make-up skills, and wondered how soon he'd be bored by her talking about work and country walks and her penchant for coffee and antique shops and food and, well, not an awful lot else...

CHAPTER FOUR

AND SO IT STARTED!

As a mug of coffee was plonked by Lina's bed, instead of wandering out, as she usually did, Shona hovered.

'Something smells good,' Lina commented, because there were gorgeous herby scents coming from their kitchen.

'Duck in plum sauce,' Shona said. 'It's in the slow cooker.'

'You made it?'

'Of course I didn't. Not that I'll tell Marcus that—you have to give yourself every advantage.'

'What happens when he finds out that you can't boil an egg?'

'He'll never find out, not if I can help it. What time are you going out?'

'Seven.' Lina yawned. 'What time's Marcus coming?'

'He should be home around then.'

Lina felt her nostrils pinch at Shona's choice of word. This wasn't his home, but as Shona sat down on the edge of the bed, Lina knew what was coming. 'You know his lease is up in a couple of months…'

'Shona,' Lina said, and closed her eyes. 'Can I just have my coffee…?'

'Sure.'

As Shona flounced out, Lina's knew that her own hackles were up and she didn't want them to be up tonight. She wanted to just enjoy looking forward to her first date with Garth, not focus on the upcoming expiration of Marcus's lease, and the inevitable conversations to be had.

Except there would be no enjoying tonight because not two minutes later her phone buzzed and she saw that it was Garth. 'Lina, you have no idea how much I hate to do this.'

'You're cancelling.' Lina said it for him, as her face pinched with disappointment.

'I'm working,'

'You're not.' She was her usual direct self. 'You told May you were unpacking this weekend.'

'I did, but I have a colleague who's having a bit of a rough time of it and I've just come off a long conversation with them and agreed to shadow them, which means I'm following their roster.'

'Oh.' He mentioned no name and gave nothing to indicate to whom he was referring, but Lina knew it was Huba. 'I'm suspicious by nature.' She gave a half-smile. 'Comes with the job…'

And with her dating life, Lina thought but didn't add.

'So,' Garth was practical, 'let's reschedule…'

Only the off-duty gods had it in for them: Lina was back on days and he wasn't off until her weekend away, with one exception. He told her about a jazz café near him, and said that he could *try* and get tickets for that trio she liked who were playing on Friday.

'Sorry?' Lina frowned. What trio that she liked?

'When I drove you home…'

'Oh!' The ones who felt like having root-canal treatment. Yet, while she wasn't into jazz, she was terribly into him and so she agreed.

'I am sorry about tonight.'

'It's fine,' Lina said.

It was and it wasn't.

'He cancelled?' Shona frowned as she came off the phone.

'It's no big deal.'

Shona wasn't so sure. 'Your very first date and he cancelled? Doesn't bode well, if you ask me.'

Lina hadn't asked, but even so it left that niggle of doubt wriggling in her stomach.

She felt dumped before they had even started.

He *had* let her down, Garth knew that, but he'd had little choice. And even if he couldn't fully explain the reason to Lina, it was the right thing to do because by Friday he could feel Huba's confidence returning.

'You're starting to get on my nerves.' Huba laughed, and so did he as they came out from seeing a patient.

He took no offence. 'That's the plan.'

It had been a good week workwise and he was looking forward to tonight, though he was rather sure May was onto him as she'd heard him earlier in the week, trying to get two tickets to the jazz café, and it had proved rather difficult. 'Any plans for the weekend?' she, oh, so casually asked.

'Some,' Garth said. 'Though I'll come in tomorrow for a few hours and try and get through some paperwork.'

'So not really here?' May checked.

'Not really here,' Garth agreed, 'so don't

go adding me to the whiteboard. I'm hoping
that I might finally get my unpacking done.'

'Any other plans?'

'Isn't that enough to be going on with?'

May's lips pursed as she fought to find out
his real plans, but he was saved from further interrogation as Reception put through
a call to her.

'North East...' May frowned as she took
the phone then was of course all smiles and
laughed. 'Oh, I wondered what on earth you
were calling me for. Yes, Lina Edwards...'

Garth deliberately didn't turn his head,
just carried on examining an X-ray image
on his computer as he heard what a wonderful student nurse Lina had been before going
on to study paramedicine, and she chatted
on as only May could!

'She's worked here on and off for years,'
May said, and continued to sing Lina's
praises. 'I always request her if she's available, though that will have to stop if she's
in Newcastle...'

And so the glowing reference continued.

'Yes... Yes... Oh, absolutely, yes... Well,
I personally would be very sorry to lose
her...'

Garth sat there, pretending to concentrate as May basically said what he already knew—just how wonderful Lina was.

And that she was planning to go.

It rather put a dampener on tonight.

In turn, Lina too was fast losing the magic.

'You have a song!' Brendan teased as they battled rush-hour traffic to get back to base. It had been a busy week and at this rate she might not even make it back in time to go out tonight.

'Yes.' Lina rolled her eyes as they sat at traffic lights. 'We haven't been out yet but we have a song, only I don't know what it is or who it's by…'

She hadn't told Brendan directly about Garth, or rather that her date was a doctor at The Primary, and he was distracted enough by his very pregnant wife to miss that the details were sketchy, and just assumed that it was someone she'd met online.

'But he cancelled on you last week?'

'Yep.'

Lina did not want to get into it with Brendan, especially after Shona's little sniff and doom and gloom forecast.

'Did he say why?'

'Work,' Lina answered, 'and if we don't

get a move on I'm going to have to do the same to him.'

It was ten to six by the time she got home and doubts were pinging as rapidly as Shona's suggestions as to what she should wear.

'You can't wear jeans!'

'I've looked it up,' Lina said, running out of the shower wrapped in a towel and carefully selecting her absolute favourite underwear—the most gorgeous satin in kingfisher blue. And truly it wasn't selected with Garth in mind, it just made her feel fantastic when she was wearing it. 'It's casual,' she explained to Shona. 'Well, there's a dressier bit upstairs but we won't be at that…' She hoped not as, aside from the expense, downstairs there were club sandwiches and a craft beer she was hoping to try.

'But don't you want him to think you've made an effort? I mean, you wear jeans to the shops, jeans everywhere really, when you're not at work.'

Lina held her breath.

Shona was actually really nice, but they clearly weren't destined to spend the rest of their lives living together. That was the trouble with flatmates, Lina had found: you got close, too close.

Shona would be a brilliant friend, if she didn't live in the same rather cosy space.

'I could wear the grey pinafore…' Lina said, running out of time as she searched through her wardrobe.

'Your interview outfit?' Shona scoffed. 'Try that dress of mine I told you about…'

'It's too much,'

'Lina, it really isn't.'

The trouble was, Lina liked Garth enough to try something different because what she'd done in the past had never worked.

Yes, she liked him enough to try on a violet dress that looked nice with black tights and flat shoes. She would wear her hair down for the first time in for ever and put on a slick of mascara too.

'I've got a nice trench coat…' Shona was enjoying herself now, and it was nice to chat and have a laugh. 'You look fantastic,' Shona said, and in truth it looked nicer than Lina had expected, although she wasn't sure about the clunky necklace that Shona had also loaned her. 'Is he picking you up?'

'No, the café is near his place.'

'And it's jazz?'

'Modern jazz,' Lina said, 'I think.' She honestly had no clue and that was *after* looking the trio up!

And then, just when she was thinking that Shona really wasn't that bad, and that maybe things would sort themselves out, *it* started up again…

It being the tricky topic of Marcus.

'Don't answer yet,' Shona said, 'but how would you feel about Marcus moving in?

As Lina opened her mouth to unfollow instructions and answer, Shona hurried to speak. 'It would help out with the rent, and he works shifts so…' Her voice trailed off. 'Just think about it.'

Lina had been thinking about it for weeks—it was the reason after all that she had an interview lined up in Newcastle.

She was so sick and tired of sharing.

The flat was gorgeous but seriously small and the thought of three of them fighting for the bathroom… As well as that, one of the advantages of her shift work meant that there was plenty of time being here on her own. Marcus was a shift worker too, so that would put paid to that.

As well as that, *she* had found the flat.

It should be Shona moving out rather than Marcus moving in.

The tube rattled her, a little late and a whole lot frazzled, towards her destination. Lina further wound herself up with the dread of Marcus moving in until, two stops from her destination, she caught sight of her reflection. She hardly recognised herself and took the chunky necklace off.

It was too much. She just felt all wrong and awkward, and now she was annoyed about Marcus too.

Somehow she made it just on time.

'Hey.' Garth smiled and they shared a brief kiss, which made everything feel a bit better.

'How was your week?' he asked as they walked to the venue. 'Has your partner had his baby?'

'No, we're still on baby watch,' Lina said. 'How was yours?'

'It was good,' Garth said, but he didn't add that it had been good up until this afternoon when he'd heard she was thinking of leaving.

He knew it was none of his business, and that it was not a subject he could broach, but the news that she was potentially leaving had put a slight pall over him, which he was doing his level best to shrug off.

It was hardly Lina's fault that he'd found out, Garth had repeatedly told himself.

And also it was so nice to see her again.

They stepped into a very nice bar with

a stage and gallery with tables where it seemed things were more formal.

Jeans would have been fine down here, Lina soon realised as she looked around. She tugged the dress down as she suddenly felt all awkward and just not herself.

'I've got us a table up there but shall we have a drink at the bar first?' Garth suggested, and her heart sank just a little.

'Sure.'

Lina ordered wine instead of the craft beer she really wanted to try.

She usually tried not to care what others thought, but she rather liked him, and tonight seemed to be about trying something different.

'I am sorry about last week—' Garth said as their drinks arrived.

'Honestly, it's fine,' Lina cut in. 'My flatmate, Shona, thought I was out for the night and had planned a romantic night in. I had to wear earplugs.'

He laughed. They were just finding themselves again, just starting to chat, when it was time to head up to their table. It really wasn't the best place for a first date because, while the food was fantastic, she'd honestly have preferred a club sandwich, and the music was just so loud and so...

…unfamiliar.

It was like an awkward 'met online' date and despite playing them down to Brendan, Lina had had plenty. Still, at least he didn't disappear on her before the first course was served, which she took as a plus. Finally, there was an interval in the music while the band took a break.

'Great, aren't they?' Garth said as the waiter topped up her wine.

'Loud!' Lina said, and then corrected herself. 'But yes…' Well, what could she say? Maybe she could get into the music if Garth wasn't sitting there, but he was so completely distracting—in the very nicest of ways. He smelt all soapy, as he had on the night they'd met, and though he hadn't shaved it was clear he'd had a shower. She liked the scent of him as they leaned across the table to catch what each other was saying.

'May's been trying to get out of me who I'm out with tonight. She overheard me ordering the tickets.'

'May's a white witch,' Lina explained, and Garth nodded.

'I had rather worked that out. She made it look as if I was volunteering information when I told her I'd moved, but she'd have known anyway from the emergency contact list being updated...'

'That's May.' Lina smiled. She thought about May's offer to speak with her about her upcoming decision. She looked over at Garth and considered mentioning it, but why spoil the night by bringing up her tentative plans?

'Do you ever think of going back to nursing?' he asked. Little did Lina know that he was inching towards giving her an opening, hoping that she'd tell him of the plans that she clearly carried in her mind.

'No.' Lina shook her head. 'I love being out on the road,' she admitted. 'Especially night shifts. Sometimes, early in the morning, I feel as I've got London all to myself. Well, apart from Brendan and the patient and ambulance control...'

She made him smile.

And she made him think, because here he sat, wanting more information from her. Yet Garth inwardly acknowledged that he hadn't shared the biggest piece of himself either.

He looked down towards the stage. The band was coming back on and soon the relative peace would be gone. But because there was noise and chatter and laughter, it really wasn't the time to just spill out your past.

And so they went back to silence and to being somewhat awkward until the band finished playing.

'Another drink?' Garth offered, but it felt like a polite offer rather than a heartfelt one and Lina was rather certain that the night was already done.

'Not for me.'

They were all polite smiles as she pulled on Shona's trench coat and he paid the undoubtedly vast bill, refusing her offer to go halves. Even if she couldn't really afford it, Lina liked to pay her way, especially as it must have been an expensive night.

As they stepped outside, Lina was rather certain she was heading for the tube and home—or, worse, a really awkward, long car-ride. It was all such a let-down...

'They were great,' Lina said. 'Thanks, though I wish you'd let me pay.'

'Why?' Garth said. 'I asked you. And, yes, they were great, but it wasn't the best choice... It wasn't the best place to talk.'

'No,' she agreed, and fully expected him to politely thank her for a lovely night and then make his excuses and walk away, or see her to the station. Except he didn't walk away, and he didn't make his excuses to leave, as so many had before.

Instead he told her what was on his mind. 'It was possibly the most stupid place to take someone you want to get to know…' Lina blinked in surprise and looked up and then smiled some more when he said, 'And I do want to get to know you some more.'

So he wasn't just walking away.

'How about a coffee, then?' Lina said, and even though the sky was black and heavy it felt as if the sun had come out.

'I'd like that very much.'

It didn't matter where, just that they both wanted to be there. They sat in a tiny café on plastic seats—her treat this time, but it had long ago stopped being about the bill.

It was terrible coffee, and stale end-of-day baklava, but the company was back to being divine. In fact, their little plastic seats were side by side as she showed him the route she'd mapped out for her days off.

'It looks amazing,' Garth said. His days off had been spent moving and putting off unpacking and then there had been a couple of hellish days in Wales. How much better it might have been had he thought to plan a couple of days walking, either side of that visit. 'Have you stayed at any of these?' he asked.

'No. I just look at reviews,' Lina said.

'There's a bit of pot luck involved. I splurged with this one…' she pulled up the listing of the tiny hotel '…and got a room with a kettle *and* biscuits.'

'Living dangerously.'

This bad date had just got a whole lot better—though some would say worse because as they stepped out of the café the heavens suddenly opened. There wasn't even a first drop of rain to warn of the impending cloudburst, no warning shower. Instead, there was just a sudden and heavy downpour that had people yelping and dashing into doorways, but she just laughed as he gripped her hand and they ran.

There was water pouring out of the drains and down the pavement, cascading down the stairs into the tube station, but they ran past that too, and she was like no woman he knew because she was laughing and laughing.

No, a bit of rain didn't worry her. She'd seen far worse at work. But although it was fun, and exhilarating, they were soon drenched and cold.

Drenched and in a doorway and wet and… suddenly sexy.

He kissed her hard and she had never felt such violent attraction before.

And as for thunder, it was a paltry effort compared to the power of his hungry kiss.

They didn't need food, or music, or even conversation; they both just needed this...

His hands were inside her coat and she was shivering not with the cold but with want. He simply turned her on in a way no other man had.

But they had to stop—they were trying to stop, to slow down, lest he take her in a doorway, and of course that wasn't going to happen...

'Shall we make a run for it?' Lina suggested. From memory, his flat was five minutes away.

It was a mad run because her shoes went all floppy and she ended up taking them off, and then piggy-backing on him. But it was not to his basement garage he took her to this time—instead it was the agony of an elevator when they both wanted to be in bed.

Shona's stupid coat really was just for appearances as it was totally impractical. As they fell through his door, she was drenched, right down to the thick black tights and azure knickers that she was peeling off while their lips meshed together...

And Garth, who was usually the most sensible person—boring almost, when it came to sexual health—was trying and failing to reach for a condom as she grappled with his zipper and took him out.

Her wet, cold hand should have doused his ardour a fraction but so urgent was their need for each other that he was pressing her against the wall instead.

Lina had never been kissed so hard, so completely deliciously, in her life before, and there was *nothing* tender about the way she kissed him back.

And then he was lifting her, and he took her against the wall, so perfectly that she arched her back and clung on with her legs. It might be *his* neighbours who needed the earplugs tonight!

'Garth!' she was shouting.

'Not yet,' he warned as he thrust into her and *told* her she couldn't come yet …

For Lina, who normally had to chase her orgasm or—whisper—fake it, and who had never once been required to hold onto it, what a delicious demand that was. She was taut all over and grinding down on him, loving his strength and the pressure of his hands as he held her.

But soon there could be no more holding on because it was coursing through her, and if he hadn't been holding her down, Lina was sure she would have shot out of his arms because he groaned, such a pure earthy groan, as he found his release. A sound came from her throat, one she had never heard before. It was a sort of sob, or a cry, as he coaxed out the last flickers of her orgasm with his own.

He lowered her down slowly and they stood there, heads together and sated. She was so disorientated from the intensity that for a moment she didn't actually know where she was. Her eyes opened to a shadowy room, lit only by the streetlight outside and containing just boxes. As she reached for a sidelight, his hand caught hers. 'Don't turn on the lights.'

'What?' Lina snapped. Suddenly, there was a tiny frisson of fear, because she had, after all, just had sex against a wall with a stranger.

Only he wasn't a stranger—it was Garth. And then she laughed as he admitted, 'I haven't got curtains yet.'

They had a quick tidy up before he turned on the light.

'You really haven't unpacked.' Lina blinked as she looked around.

'No. I swore I'd have everything put away before I started back at work but it's...' He halted and Lina had the feeling that something had been left unsaid. 'I've got a table and couches being delivered but not for another fortnight...'

'It's really gorgeous,' she said as she looked up at the high ceilings.

'But cold. The heating isn't working yet. Well, it is but it's not particularly warm.'

'Maybe the radiators need bleeding,' Lina suggested, and then stopped herself. Suggesting things was something else she tended to do a lot and it never went down well.

'You're probably right,' Garth said. 'I should have thought of that.'

He led her through to his bedroom but, given that there were only sheets up at the windows and not very well secured, he took her through to the bathroom to strip off for bed.

There they undressed, both seeing what they'd just explored and still delighted with each other. Lina smiled approvingly. He really was utterly beautiful, she thought as she traced her fingers down his chest, and that stubbly unshaven jaw was as black as the hair on his chest. She liked the feel of it as she touched it but then she just stood, arms lifted, as he took off her wet dress.

'Do you know...?' he said as he got to her fantastic underwear. 'I didn't expect this...'

'I love underwear...' she breathed, delighted that he approved of the stunning kingfisher-blue satin she had selected with such care.

'No, this,' he told her, and she looked down. 'Lina, you're purple.'

She was!

'That bloody dress!' The dye had leaked and she had been turned purple! Now they were both sort of hysterical with quiet laughter. 'I knew I should have stuck to jeans...'

'I'm going to bathe you...'

'I haven't had a bath in...' She couldn't actually remember how long.

'I've even got this...' He opened a huge cellophane-wrapped basket. 'Housewarming gift,' he explained as he took out oils and candles.

'Who's that from?'

'My friend Boris and his partner...'

She was smiling as he ran the bath because he was so unfamiliar with it all that he had to read the instructions on the bubble bath!

'More than that!' Lina said as he carefully measured out two lids full. She took over running the bath as he wrapped a towel round himself and headed off to look for glasses and wine.

Yes, the lack of a condom needed to be discussed—and it would be—but… Garth didn't know what was happening between them. It wasn't just the incredible sex, but it had never been so intense, not since…

He shut down that thought process quickly but then as he opened the fridge he was blinded with insight rather than light.

It was because she was leaving, he decided. That was why it felt so insanely intense between them.

Not that she'd told him she was.

But maybe that was what allowed him to be a bit freer with her.

Garth hadn't had a bath since who knew when either, and certainly not a candlelit one with bubbles and wine.

'It's Shona's dress,' Lina explained as he climbed in.

'We should send her a thank-you card,' Garth said as the water engulfed them and they washed each other.

'And to Boris.'

'Indeed,' he agreed. 'If you'd have come tomorrow that basket would have been forgotten in a cupboard or at the Oxfam shop.'

This was them; they were back to the

fun and ease that naturally existed between them. They talked between kisses. Yes, she was on the Pill and, no, neither usually went without protection. It had been an anomaly for them both, and one that would hopefully soon be repeated, but for now they just talked lazily, filling in gaps... 'It turned out that it wasn't a casual affair,' she said when he asked about her dad. 'They're married now. He lives there.'

'Do you see much of him?'

'No,' Lina said. 'We were really close when I was younger. I was his favourite...' She gave a pale smile. 'Flights are expensive...'

He said nothing.

'And he's got a new family. Well, they're almost teenagers now...'

Still he said nothing.

In the past, so many guys had jumped in and pointed out how awful her father was, but his silence was patient, and for once she voiced her deepest thoughts.

'When he left he said that things wouldn't change, that we'd still be close, but then Sally got pregnant...' She looked at him. She didn't want to bring down the fun of their date, but he made it so easy to reach inside herself and just say what she never had. 'He could have made at least some effort.'

'Yes,' Garth said. It was the first comment he had made on the subject, but he saw the dart of pain flash in her eyes. 'But people sometimes don't want to face up to their mistakes, and I'm sure he knows he made one...'

'The marriage was already over.' Lina shook her head, assuming he was discussing her father's affair. 'Now I'm older and can understand things a little better, I can see how incompatible they were...'

'I meant perhaps he knows he made a mistake not keeping properly in touch with you.'

She looked at him.

'It's easy to let things slide,' Garth said, 'except once you have, it makes things harder to pick up. Do you think he regrets not making more of an effort with you?'

She thought for a moment. 'Maybe.' She nodded. 'He's always so awkward when we speak, but then so am I. We used to just talk all the time. I used to be able to go to him with all my problems...'

He kissed her sad mouth, but not to stop her from talking. In fact, it opened her up.

'I miss him,' she admitted. 'He's a nice guy, and I know he hurt my mum but...'

'You are allowed to still love him.'

'Not in my family you're not,' Lina sighed. 'It's agony when he's here. He came back for Daniel's wedding...'

'Daniel?'

'My brother, the older one. It was all so awkward. I mean, *so* awkward... My mum was furious with him still, and both families together...' She closed her eyes at the tension of it and then opened them to his amazing navy ones that were just the nicest thing to look at. 'You read all about these access battles and...' She shrugged. 'Not my dad. I hate it that he didn't even pretend to put up a fight for me.' And there was no real answer to that, so she asked about him. 'What about your family?'

'There's just my dad.'

'Do you get on?'

'We do.' He nodded, and seemed to think about it for a moment. 'He's coming to see the flat next weekend and I believe he's bringing a friend.'

'A friend?'

'Terrible when your parents are dating, isn't it?'

They both laughed and then stopped laughing and found themselves looking into each other's eyes.

'Come to bed,' he told her. She was no longer purple, and the water was cooling off, but more importantly he just had to have her all over again.

Afterwards they lay there, both holding their breath as if waiting for the magic to disperse…except it didn't.

She had never felt so uninhibited with another person, so into another person, and unashamedly so.

They lay there till the heat from their lovemaking left them cool and they shivered as they turned and faced each other.

'If I sleep,' Garth warned, 'I'm going to really sleep.'

'One of the perks of my job—' Lina smiled '—is that I can sleep on demand.'

It was bliss to lie in his bed, to listen to the hum of traffic outside and the pelting rain on the windows, and to know that they had to be nowhere other than here.

'I think I'm going to get drapes the exact shade of your underwear,' he said, and smiled right into her eyes.

'Kingfisher-blue.' Lina smiled back. 'I didn't wear them just for you. I always have gorgeous underwear on.'

'I'll try not to bear that in mind when you bring a patient in.'

'My knicker drawer is like a jewellery box.'
'Really?'

It was her one stab at femininity, the one thing she held onto, and she told him so. 'My mum—and I adore her, by the way—is the dizziest, vaguest... Well, let's just say housework was never her forte...'

He smiled as she spoke, and it was nice to lie in a freezing room and be warm and chatting sleepily.

'So there were never neat piles of washing to put away, it was just a jumble in the airing cupboard.

'I did my own,' Garth said. 'Well, when I was back from boarding school.'

'Oh, stop with the sob story,' Lina said, smiling. 'At least you didn't have to suffer my fate.'

'Which was?'

'Well, the wind blew my school dress up and I was wearing a pair of my brother's Spiderman Y-fronts.'

They laughed and laughed and laughed. She had never done that before, Lina realised, just lain in bed laughing with a man. And then Garth paused, and it was as if, for a moment, he was thinking exactly the same thing.

'So, when I got a job, and pocket money,

from the very day I could buy my own un-derwear I bought the prettiest, brightest, girliest underwear I could, and to this day it persists.'

'I'm very glad to hear it.'

Just before he fell asleep he gave a low laugh, and with her head on her chest she simply knew he was thinking about an eight-year-old Lina in Spiderman Y-fronts, and her most embarrassing moment suddenly didn't burn quite so much.

She felt understood.

Better, she felt completely herself.

It was, she decided, a rather nice place to be.

CHAPTER FIVE

RAIN, RAIN, GO AWAY...

Except they both kind of liked the sound as they woke up in their freezing cocoon, all bundled under the blankets and knotted together. But reality—and their busy schedules—was starting to invade.

'I swore I'd go in and lock myself in my office.' Garth yawned. 'I have a mountain of paperwork after this week...'

'Shadowing?' She didn't say Huba's name and she wondered if he would, but it was a little early to be sharing professional confidences.

'Yes,' Garth said. 'I wanted to get some stuff out of the way before the start of the week, but—'

'Go in,' Lina interrupted, and told him about the *latest* organisation book that she'd been reading, of which she'd amassed quite a collection. 'You'll feel better for it. Well, according to my book. You don't have to do it all, just make a start, but the chances are that once you get going you won't want to stop.'

'I *will* want to stop if I know you're waiting for me here.'

Lina blinked.

She'd rather expected a *Thanks for a great night, but*…followed by a cold journey home on the tube—or rather a damp and cold journey, given that Shona's purple dress and underwear were lying in a puddle on the bathroom floor.

Except it would seem that, like her, Garth didn't want it to end just yet either.

'Well,' Lina slowly admitted, as she didn't want to appear too eager and terrify him, 'I *am* avoiding Shona.'

'Your flatmate? Why?'

'She's hoping to have "a talk".' Her hands lifted and she made the quotation marks, but then, given the icy air, she shot them back under the covers and toyed with his lovely chest hair as she spoke on. 'She wants her partner to move in with us.'

He pulled a suitably distasteful face and Lina gave a soft laugh.

'I feel the same way.'

'So say no.'

'It's more complicated than that…' It was Lina's turn to yawn. She wasn't avoiding a conversation, but it was also far too early in the morning to be going into the drama of Shona and Marcus and the ongoing saga of living arrangements.

And Garth understood that she wasn't avoiding talking or anything, simply that she was tired. 'Stay if you like,' Garth said. 'I'll bring food back, though I've no idea when.'

'Sounds wonderful.'

'There's a set of spare keys on the mantelpiece if you need to go out, but don't try and start the unpacking…'

'Oh, please.' Lina laughed. 'I'm no domestic goddess, if that's what you're hoping for.'

'No.' He hadn't meant it like that; it was more the piles and piles of boxes that he needed to go through alone. It was something Garth had been putting off, yet now it felt like something he might be ready to start tackling—perhaps he should ask for the name of that book she'd been reading. 'Just rest up, and I'll be back as soon as I can. Do you want a drink before I head off?'

'Not now.' Lina was more than happy to head straight back to sleep.

They shared a lazy kiss and Garth was

soon headed out with his tea in a keep-cup, leaving Lina dozing in bed.

And what usually would seem unfathomable—to leave someone in his bed and head to work—felt normal and right.

Invigorating even?

Because for once the pile of paperwork waiting for him felt like something to get through briskly rather than a burden that would stretch out all day.

Lina had no idea when he'd be back and it mattered not; it was just nice to have space, even if wasn't her own. She couldn't find coffee but made a cup of tea instead. The contents of his fridge weren't exactly enthralling, but she was high on last night rather than hungry this morning, and his flat really was freezing.

So freezing that she had another bath just to warm up, and then found a T-shirt of his to put on while she threw Shona's violet dress and her tights over a very tepid radiator, even though the heating was up on high.

Ah, yes! His radiators.

Not your problem.

Lina reminded herself of the guy who'd told her she'd emasculated him by changing his tyre but, hell, it was freezing.

And anyway, she doubted Garth Hughes was capable of being emasculated and so she set to work.

Hanging on the radiator in the lounge room, she found the key, and a couple of hours were spent bleeding the radiators into a Tupperware container she'd unearthed. And it worked, so much so that by the time she was working on the one in the bathroom the place was so warm that she had to turn the heating down!

Then there were another couple of glorious hours lying in bed, just scrolling through the news—all without the sound of Marcus and Shona bonking, or having a row, or knocking on her door and asking if she had a charger they could *borrow*, or if she minded if they used the bacon and they'd get some next time they hit the shops, or Shona wanting to have 'the talk'…

Mind you, a good part of those couple of hours were spent thinking about Garth…

Oh, there was history in those boxes, Lina was absolutely sure. After all, she still hadn't worked out the reason he was mid-thirties, gorgeous and single, but not once was she tempted to snoop.

It was all too new and too shiny and precious, and she didn't need to go looking for a pin to pop their little bubble.

And so when he texted and said he was stuck for the foreseeable future with a broken ankle, she texted back not to worry about grabbing food because she'd sort it.

The violet dress and black tights were far too much for the high street, but she covered them in Shona's coat and was too delighted to care.

Lina bought some dips and fried mozzarella sticks, and ready-made samosas and tiny sausage rolls, as well as some wine. And, given the month, she bought some discounted Christmas pudding, and ready-made custard too. It was all a mish-mash of deliciousness. Certainly there was no domestic goddess involved, or duck in plum sauce that she'd disguised as her own. After the dress debacle, Lina was more determined than ever to simply be herself.

Her damp clothes were back drying on the radiator when he texted to say that he was on his way, and she set up for an indoor picnic.

And Garth, who'd been working up to having a 'talk' of his own—perhaps even opening up about his past—walked into a toasty warm apartment to find Lina in his

T-shirt and a blanket spread out on his floor covered in plates and finger food.

'Are we having a party?' he asked.

'Sort of,' Lina said. 'Well, this is my version of a gourmet dinner. All the best bits, without the knives and forks.'

The difficult conversation he had been planning to have flew out of the window. He'd forgotten the feeling of coming home to someone and just stood taking it in for a moment. 'We need candles,' Garth finally said.

Thank goodness for Boris and his basket of goodies because soon they were sitting on the rug with last night's candles set on various saucers and flickering in the low light.

It was romantic, it was fun, but more than that it was all so simple to lie back, completely full, and just look at the high ceilings and the ribbons of light from the melting candles, and listen to the traffic in the wet streets below and talk about, well, not much.

'My flat's so tiny,' Lina said. 'You could paint the ceiling lying down. You'd need a crane to do yours.'

'I might just stick to candlelight,' Garth said, and that made them smile. 'So Marcus wants to move into your tiny flat?'

'Correction,' Lina said, 'I think the hope is that I'll move out. It's a brilliant flat.' She explained the complicated unwritten rules. 'It's actually got a little balcony off the fire escape that's covered, and it's got plants and everything.'

'Sounds good.' He nodded.

'It's perfect,' Lina replied. 'You can sit out there in summer without having to go down to a park, it's just so nice. And I was the one who found it.'

'I see.'

'I lived there for two years before Shona.'

'So she should be the one to move out?' he checked.

'Yes, but who needs a disgruntled flat-mate?' They looked at each other. 'Not me.'

'No.'

'But I just can't be bothered finding an-other flatmate and sharing again...' She stopped herself, lest she reveal her plans.

Except that little bone of contention that had niggled since he'd heard May on the phone faded then as he realised she was possibly just working through her options. 'What did you tell Shona?'

'That I'm thinking about it,' Lina said. 'Which I'll do on my trip. I do all my think-ing when I walk. Well, my big thinks.'

'I need to do that,' Garth said. 'Allocate my thinking.'

'You should.' And she told him about another book she'd read—or was it a podcast?—but they never really got to the bottom of it because Lina was precariously close to suggesting he join her on her trip and Garth was wondering what Richard's reaction would be if he suddenly asked for the next weekend off.

It was safer to get dessert.

'What is it?' Garth asked as the microwave whirred again.

'Don't look.' She turned out the pudding, and while she was warming up the custard she opened the tiny miniature of brandy she had bought and poured it over the pudding and set fire to it. 'Okay, you can look now...'

Garth didn't know where to look first.

The dancing blue light on the Christmas pudding, her bare legs walking towards him, the way she smiled as she carried it over... This Saturday night was up there with the best he had known.

'Christmas pudding...' he said as she put the plate down and he watched its fading flames as she headed off for the custard. 'I don't—'

'Don't tell me you don't like Christmas pudding!' Lina warned.

'I love Christmas pudding,' he corrected.

'I was going to say that I haven't had it in years.'

'Why not?' She was aghast at the very thought and Garth found he couldn't tell her that Christmas had been placed on hold in recent years, because he didn't want to bring this perfect night to a screeching halt. She made him laugh and smile, and it would change things to start talking about sad things. Selfishly maybe, he just didn't want to go there right now.

'I just…' He didn't finish and didn't explain because right now he wanted to hold onto this little bit of magic and *ease* that she had brought to him.

Not that Lina noticed his silence. 'I live off it in January,' she told him, 'and mince pies…'

Lina knelt up, at first to reach for the custard, but when he caught her wrist and she looked into his eyes her sweet tooth was completely forgotten.

'Thank you for this,' Garth said.

'You mean my amazing microwave skills?'

'I adore your microwave skills,' he said as his lips brushed hers. A picnic in winter and a home full of warmth—what could be better? As their lips met he ran a hand along her naked thigh and then to her waist.

And then back down, to check something he might have missed, but, no, her knickers really were over the radiator. He groaned as his hand met her bare bottom.

It was not their first kiss together—after all, they had been entwined often since last night—but this was the first kiss for them both where time seemed to stop, where they actually met, because it was such a slow and deeply intimate kiss. They both opened their eyes just to witness the other's pleasure.

He scooped her towards him, and though a tiny plate of mini sausage rolls was knocked over courtesy of her foot, it was of such little significance that it didn't merit either a look or an interruption to acknowledge it. Instead, she sat on his lovely solid thighs and stared into his face and wondered how the hell she could ever have considered him grumpy because Garth Hughes was simply too delicious for words.

She approached his open heart with ease and did not even have to check her words as she spoke, for he accepted her.

'You need curtains,' she told him as she stared into navy eyes, and he pulled her indecently close so that he pressed into her.

'I know,' Garth acknowledged, and he kissed her again, because it was so much easier to do than to get up right now. But somehow, and with mammoth effort, he unlatched their locked lips and peeled them apart. He stood up, holding his hand out to help her up.

'You really, really need curtains,' Lina grumbled as they made their dash to the privacy of the sheeted windows in his bedroom.

'First thing on my list,' Garth said when they got there. 'No, second,' he said as he peeled off her T-shirt—which was actually his, but neither cared right now.

'What's first?' a naked Lina asked as she pressed her body against his clothed one and kissed him as if it was the most essential, necessary, most vital thing in the world.

'You are.'

For Garth it was as if the sky had split open and the air was suddenly clear because for this blissful time there was nothing on his mind other than Lina.

Nothing other than her skin, and how necessary it was to undress himself so that every inch of him could be pressed against every inch of her.

He stripped and she laughed in delight and called him a magician, because one minute there was a belt and socks and a tie to contend with and the next, his body was hers to behold and hold and together they tumbled onto the unmade bed.

Yes, unmade, because she was no domestic goddess, but who cared? Not Garth.

He made her skin tingle and the weight of him pinning her down made her feel tiny when she was certainly not.

His jaw was rough on her skin and his hands were firm and she loved it. She had never known a kiss could be so exquisite and perfect as he kissed every inch of her skin.

They were just so into each other, so wanting each other. She lay back as he kissed her all over then rolled her over and kissed her spine. She had never known sex could be so slow and so good, or so honest.

He made her feel gorgeous by the roaming of his hands and the soft attention of his mouth.

'What are you doing to me?' she groaned.

'Hopefully the same as you're doing to me,' Garth said, and they sank into the bliss that their bodies gave to each other.

It did not feel too soon to be so adoring of him. If anything, as she lay beneath him, Lina wondered how she had survived to near thirty without knowing the bliss of being properly made love to. Oh, he wasn't her first, but he was the first to make her feel as important and as cherished. This was how it should be.

His body was warm under her hands and she was just this knot of hot desire. The scratch of his jaw on her cheek felt sublime, and he panted into her ear as he entered her.

Oh, where were the condoms? she thought as he thrust into her, but then she remembered that they were past all that. They were in this place, without vocal discussion, where they were here together, and it was just them.

They were locked in an embrace and in a place where no one else would be invading.

'I raced.' he said as he took her higher.

'Tell me,' she said as she dug into his buttocks with her stubby fingers that had chewed nails, but in her mind she was dizzy as she galloped alongside his chain of thought.

'To get through it...'

'I know,' she gasped, because she knew that today he had been on fast forward to get through his paperwork and it excited her, it *excited* her, that she had been on his mind all day. 'I was the same.' This delicious day had been all about filling her trolley with goodies for them and the thought of a night with him.

'I wanted…' She wanted to tell him how she'd wished to turn the hands on the clock, just so it could be now, but words had left her because he took her so deeply and so intently, and there was nothing in the world she could focus on now other than the pounding of her senses and the absolute certainty that she could hold on no longer.

Her head was to the side, just trying to breathe for a second, to hold onto the surge that was flooding her body, to relish this solemn man and the sudden abandonment of anything else but this moment with a mutual lack of restraint.

Finally, she could hold it no more, and her climax arrived so spectacularly that he drowned in her pulsing body and the tension of her limbs. When she sank in relief and was pliant beneath him, he took her so hard against the pillow that it felt as if she had melted and she had the succinct pleasure of watching and feeling the rush of his come.

It made her want to weep because it felt so sublime—and so did the long, slow kisses afterwards as they tried to gather their breath. And then came a blissful minute of silence. Garth was still on top and inside her, and they stared at each-other in wonder.

It was the most treasured, intimate moment of her life.

For Lina, it blew every previous pathetic attempt at a relationship out of the water.

For Garth, it felt as if he'd climbed onto a life raft.

It was beyond words or logical thought.

And then they rolled apart and lay there smiling to themselves before Garth got up and, wrapping a towel around his hips, retrieved the essentials.

Cold Christmas pudding and custard had never tasted so good.

CHAPTER SIX

WHY, WHEN LIFE felt so close to perfect that she could almost reach out and touch it, could Lina not sleep?

Garth lay beside her, and though her body was all floaty and relaxed, her mind remained wide awake. Was it just the buzz of adrenaline in her veins, as she replayed the best weekend she had ever known, that kept her from drifting off? Or was it a stupid question that kept popping in uninvited as she lay there: why hadn't he had Christmas pudding in years?

It had her frowning into the darkness as she tried to answer it.

Maybe he worked each Christmas, Lina reasoned. After all, a lot of health workers did, and she had certainly done her share of working through the festivities.

Except, no matter how unsociable the hours of her work were, there was always a

Christmas dinner and pudding and all the trimmings waiting for her at her mum's, even if she didn't get there till Boxing Day. She hadn't been able to get there until New Year's Eve once! Yet they had still had their own little celebration.

Maybe it was just her family, Lina thought.

Perhaps others didn't cling onto those traditions so fiercely…

Not quite satisfied with her own answer, Lina lay there, still unable to sleep but bathed in the streetlight that came in through the sheet. She didn't mind being awake in the least. The world hadn't felt so right in a very long while and she didn't want to miss a moment, for it felt too good to be true.

Too good to last?

She disregarded that thought, simply shrugged it off and put it down to the eternal pessimist that resided within her. Well, she wasn't listening to that voice tonight. Instead, she listened to the swish of cars below and the soft sound of Garth asleep by her side.

He even *breathed* nicely for someone who was asleep on their back.

She wanted to reach out and touch his flat stomach, to wake him up in the nicest of ways. She was smiling to herself at the thought of that as she looked at his gorgeous features.

But then it happened again, that flash of recognition: she knew him. Lina was sure of it.

Oh, where had she seen that profile before?

She had felt it that first night they'd met when she'd walked into the staffroom and seen him sleeping upright in the chair—a jolt of recognition had shot through her.

And now it was happening again.

The straight aquiline nose, lips slightly parted...

It was like trying to recall a dream, Lina thought as she turned on her side and raised herself onto one elbow.

A car's lights cut through a gap between the sheet and the window and cast a sudden, fleeting flash of light on his face...

But instead of the white light flashing into the bedroom, for a moment there Lina saw blue. Or rather she recalled seeing that gorgeous face momentarily lit by blue emergency lights, then red...and she wished at that moment that she had never tried to chase the memory of his face because suddenly she remembered. She remembered him, and it was awful.

Her breathing started to come too fast and too shallow and she rather hurriedly turned onto her back and lay there feeling shaken, blocking her eyes with her arm, trying to forget what she had once seen.

She'd been to so many accidents, but there were some that stood out more than most and that were etched into her memory.

Garth hadn't been her patient, though.

Her patient had been his wife...

CHAPTER SEVEN

'COACH VERSUS MULTIPLE VEHICLES...' Wendy said.

Wendy was driving along the hard shoulder of the wet motorway with lights blazing and sirens blaring as updates came in. A major incident had been declared and Lina's pulse was rapid, her head trying to slow down and go through all she had learned as this was her first major incident.

'Jesus...' Wendy said as she slowed down on approach, and Lina quietly swallowed.

There was a coach and cars all knotted together, and dazed people walking around the motorway, being shepherded by emergency workers who were starting to bring order to the chaos.

Lina and Wendy were waved through. Many first responders were already there and as she and Wendy disembarked, they were told to take over with the driver of a

CAROL MARINELLI

car, while another team dealt with the passenger.

One look at the crumpled metal told her
this was far from good and Vos, the doctor, told her the same. The steering column,
he told her grimly, was embedded in the
patient's chest and it was going to be difficult, if not impossible, to save her. Extrac-
tion crews were working on those with a
better chance of survival for now.

'You've got this,' Wendy said, and Lina
was grateful for her crewmate's encourage-
ment as they approached.

The door of the car had been ripped off
and the patient was angled terribly, but they
had already managed to get a cervical collar on her and she was attached to a monitor
with an IV line in. Wendy took over holding the bag of saline as Lina reached in to
the woman.

'Is Garth okay?' the patient begged as
Lina peered in to make her own assessment.
'Please, will someone just tell me. Please...'
she begged. 'Can you just help my husband.
He's not making a sound...'

'There's a team with him now,' Lina assured her, not even glancing over, her focus
fully on the woman who was pinned. 'It's

Carrie, isn't it?' she checked as she started to take her vitals.

'Yes.'

'I'm Lina. Carrie, I need you to listen to me. We're going to get you and your husband out just as soon as we can, but for now I need you to stay very still.'

Carrie had on long silver earrings, a silver-grey velvet dress, and red lipstick. All these things Lina noticed in great detail, because her blusher was far too garish and severe for such a very pale face, but she was so polished and elegant that Lina knew she hadn't made a mistake with her make-up. Her skin was a horrible waxy colour that concerned Lina deeply; this alone—outside the handover information—told Lina that this patient was desperately ill.

Her vitals were better than she presented, but that brought little comfort—she was young and healthy and would hold her blood pressure better than most.

'I'm just going to get another line into you,' Lina said, 'so we can give you more fluids, while—'

'Please,' she whimpered, pulling at the oxygen mask to speak more clearly. 'Tell me how my husband is. I'm a doctor, I'm not stupid...'

'Of course you're not. Carrie, keep the mask on.' Lina's voice was firm, but she did glance over towards the passenger.

'Is he dead?' Carrie asked her bluntly. 'You have to tell me the truth!'

'No, he isn't dead,' Lina told her patient, but any more than that she honestly didn't know. She took a moment to look and assess the situation for herself.

His head was resting back on the headrest, and there must be a wound in his scalp because there was blood pouring down his face. He was unconscious but breathing, and a paramedic was wrapping the head wound and flashing a pupil torch into his eyes.

'He's breathing,' Lina told Carrie. 'He has a head wound that I can see, but he's breathing.'

'Garth.' Carrie summoned her strength and ripped off the oxygen mask, calling out to him. 'I'm here.' Her frantic pale blue eyes met Lina's. 'Can he hear me, do you think?'

'I think so.' Lina wasn't one for placating people for the sake of it. This couple were both in a terrible way, but she saw his arm lift slightly to the sound of his wife's voice. 'He just moved his hand when you spoke.'

'Hold on, Garth,' she urged him, except

her voice had gone gurgly. Lina's attention left the passenger and returned to the driver.

'I'm pregnant,' Carrie told her. 'Just.'

'Okay,' Lina said, and she relayed it to Vos, who had come back for an update.

'Garth doesn't know…' Carrie cried. 'I was going to tell him tonight when we got home. I bought champagne. Oh, God…' She started to sob, but couldn't get the air in, and it turned into a rasp. 'My baby…'

'Let's take care of *you* now.' Lina sought to calm her. 'And then we'll worry about the baby. I want you to take some nice deep breaths.'

'I don't like the mask…'

Lina turned at the sound of a voice beside her. Vos was saying, 'We're going to get the passenger out now. Once he's out we can get a better angle on her. Try and keep her calm and pain free.'

There was blood spreading over her dress and pooling in her lap now and Lina knew they were losing her.

'Carrie,' Lina said calmly, replacing the mask, 'I really need you to stay calm and keep the mask on. They're just about to move Garth now.'

But Carrie wasn't following orders and

again tore off the mask. 'I love you,' she called to him. 'Garth, I love you.'

Liana saw the blue ambulance lights flash over his pale face and Lina knew that if he did wake up it would be to a world that had changed for ever.

'We're going to get you out soon,' Lina said. 'Garth's on his way to hospital now.'

'That's good.' She closed her eyes as if in relief, but then failed to open them.

'Open your eyes, Carrie,' Lina urged. 'Tell me, how's your pain?'

'No pain,' Carrie said. 'I can't really feel anything much. Please, take the mask off. I feel like I'm suffocating...'

'You need it.'

'I'm so dizzy.'

'We're getting some fluids into you,' Lina said. 'Wendy is putting another line in and we'll have you out soon.' She looked over at Wendy, who was handing her nasal prongs to use instead of the mask; they were both doing all they could to keep her comfortable. 'There,' Lina said as she put the nasal prongs on. 'Is that better?'

'Yes.' She took a couple of breaths then spoke. 'I want the same hospital as him,' she asked. 'Please.'

'I...' She was about to say that it wasn't up

to her, but Carrie just needed comfort right now. 'I'll do all I can,' Lina said.

'I want to be with him.'

'I know you do.'

'He'll hate being a patient,' Carrie said, and breathed for a moment, then she told Lina everything.

They sat on a cold, wet motorway with the traffic halted, as Lina did her best to make Carrie comfortable. The roof was being taken off another vehicle and the noise from the Jaws of Life was deafening even here, but in the pauses between the noise of the saw they talked.

'How long have you been married?'

'Two years.' Carrie closed her eyes and smiled.

'Did you have a honeymoon?'

'Maldives,' Carrie said. 'It was just us, and...'

'Tell me,' Lina said, trying to keep her warm with memories.

It was a disjointed conversation, but she kept talking and Lina kept listening as she delivered drugs and fluids.

An emergency doctor was in the passenger side now, as well as two firefighters, all trying to decide on the best method to extract her from the steering column as Lina focussed on keeping Carrie still and calm.

'My parents...' she whimpered, clearly imagining all the awful scenarios playing out. She was a doctor after all, and, unfortunately they weren't just imagined scenarios Carrie was envisaging. They were real. 'They mustn't call them. They hate the phone...'

'Let us take care of that.'

'I want Garth to tell them. Please...' She was starting to talk nonsense, how Garth had to be the one to go and tell them, even though he was probably in the resuscitation bay by now. 'They'll listen to him.'

'Carrie,' Lina said. 'We're going to start cutting soon. It's going to be noisy, but I'll stay with you the whole time. 'Carrie?' she said. 'Carrie!' More loudly this time, 'Stay with me...'

'They gave me such a wonderful childhood...'

She spoke about a pony and a tiny school and how her mum always put down what she was doing when she got home.

'It wasn't like that for him,' Carrie said.

'For Garth?'

Carrie tried to nod, but the collar prevented it. 'I'm so thirsty...'

Of course she couldn't drink but Lina asked for a water bottle, and wiped Carrie's lips and tongue. As that bright red lipstick came off, it was replaced by white lips and a white tongue. Lina ducked away for a second then so that Vos could take another look and when he stood, his face was grim. They both knew how dire this was. The only think keeping Carrie from completely bleeding out was the steering column that was buried in her chest. 'Are you all right to keep talking to her?' Vos checked.

'Yes.' She nodded as she glanced around. There were still other patients being freed, or being urgently treated in the field or in the emergency vehicles that were all lined up. There was the smell of burning rubber and petrol in the air, so she took a quick gulp of water herself and then got back to the job.

And kept talking.

Or rather Carrie kept talking, in breathy tones, as if it was imperative that she speak.

'He's like a son to them,' Carrie said.

'Garth?'

'He couldn't take it at first,' she gasped. 'His father's such a cold bastard.' She coughed and Lina saw that it was blood. She wiped it, trying not to let Carrie see as she resumed talking...

About how they'd met at medical school. How she'd been a virgin.

Lina listened to the details of a life that was ending, and did her best to be present for her.

They'd just been to her favourite restaurant—well, second favourite, because he didn't like pasta...

All the little details of her treasured life.

'I'm cold.'

'Let's wrap this round you,' Lina said, as Wendy passed her another blanket.

She told Lina everything, really, the important and the trivial and the vital parts of her world, and all in a disjointed, broken kind of way, and Lina was right there with her. They were getting a dog because he hated cats, oh, and coffee...

She told her about her first horse.

She told Lina all that mattered in her world, and she reminisced and closed her eyes.

'I hope it's a boy...' she said, her voice fading. 'Or a girl...'

'It will be beautiful,' Lina said.

'Yes.'

Carrie's eyes opened and she mouthed, 'Same hospital?'

'Yes,' Lina said, and stroked her face. 'Same hospital as Garth.'

Lina could still remember standing roadside, looking at the covering on the body still pinned by the steering column that they hadn't got out.

She'd thought of the parents in Wales, and the husband who might wake in hospital, only to be told that his beautiful wife had died.

'That was a tough one,' Wendy had said as they did their own little debrief.

'If we'd got her out maybe…'

Wendy shook her head. 'If we'd got her out then she'd have died sooner. The only thing keeping her alive was the steering wheel.'

Lina had known that, even if she'd tried to deny it to herself as she'd done her best to keep Carrie comfortable.

Vos said the same.

'If there had been a fully prepped theatre next to the motorway, the outcome would have been the same.'

'I know.'

And now, years later, Lina lay on her back, recalling with precision the desolation of the scene, and how she'd got through the rest of her shift.

Another car accident on a dark, rainy night.

A drunk driver this time; he had been fine, apart from a few cuts. She could recall the taste of her own tears at the back of her throat at the injustice of it all and knew in her heart that it wasn't her place to judge. She'd actually landed on her mother's doorstep that very morning, which had been a waste of time.

'It's part of your job, though,' Jeanette Edwards had said as she'd handed her coffee and toast, somewhat bemused by her daughter's visible distress. 'Maybe you should think of something else if it's going to upset you this much…'

'But I'm good at it,' Lina said. 'I like what I do.'

'Well, it's clearly taking its toll.'

Her mum hadn't got it then and she didn't get it now. It was a job Lina loved, even if at times it upset her. It was then she'd realised that if she was going to survive this job she somehow had to toughen the hell up.

'I've got some days off,' Lina had said. 'I might—'

'Do you want to come here for a few days?'

her mum had offered. 'We could go out, do some shopping…'

Only it wasn't retail therapy Lina had needed.

Somehow, she'd found herself walking on the stony beach at Brighton in the middle of winter, being whipped by the wind and frozen to the core, but actually, finally, able to think.

She'd been young but already a little bit beaten down by the blows her work delivered. And she had known that if this was the career she wanted to pursue, she couldn't take each case home with her—and certainly not to her mum's. And if there were shards that remained in her heart, she must learn how to hide them better.

And for years she had.

Except Garth Hughes had brought everything she'd ever buried to the surface, both the good and the bad.

Now she lay in bed with a man she barely knew, but about whom she knew so very much.

Too much.

As a sleepless night rolled by, she lay there thinking about Carrie and how beautiful she had been, and thought what a dreadful waste of life her death had been. That night had hurt Lina enough; she could not fathom Garth's hell. She lay there, recalling all the worlds that Carrie had described, all the snippets that she'd buried and never unearthed. But now that time spent with her patient on a cold, wet night all came rushing back with painful clarity.

Dawn came at last. Except things didn't look better in the cold, grey morning. To Lina, they looked a whole lot worse.

'Hey.' Garth stirred beside her and his voice broke into her thoughts. 'You're awake.'

'Yes.' Her voice came out all high and all wrong. 'Yes.' She tried to right it.

'You okay?' He frowned.

'Of course.'

She was like some gauche teenager, awkwardly regretting things—except it wasn't that. It wasn't that!

'Do you want tea?' he asked.

'Coffee,' Lina said automatically, and then added, 'Please.'

'I hope I've got some,' Garth said, and hauled himself out of bed. 'I don't really drink the stuff...'

I know you don't, Lina thought as he headed off to the kitchen.

In their brief time together, *coffee* had never come up.

She'd been too full of it back in the café and so had drunk tea, and the nights had been about wine and romance.

But now the real world was starting to arrive: their likes and dislikes…and their pasts.

Oh, God, it was all coming back, all the things Carrie had said on that cold, dark night. He loathed coffee, pasta, his dad, cats… The memories played back in her head.

And she simply didn't know what to do with what she knew.

'I had some after all.' Garth came into the bedroom then and handed her a mug of coffee.

'Thanks.'

She blew on her coffee in an effort to cool it down so she could drink it quickly and go home to think. 'I do need to get back.'

'You don't want to go and get some breakfast first? Or we can have a picnic…'

'Not for me. I really ought to go.'

'Is everything okay?' Garth checked. 'You're not…?'

'I'm fine.' Lina smiled. 'Shona's out and my cat is going to be screaming to be fed, poor thing.'

He hated cats!

Yikes.

He was a dog person, but to her surprise he didn't pull a face or declare to her that he was actually more of a canine kind of guy.

'Cat lady, me,' she said. It was the most ridiculous thing to say, but her mouth was like a runaway train. Was she testing him? No.

Maybe.

She didn't know. Her head was a jumble.

'What's his name?'

'Her,' Lina said.

'What's her name?'

'Gretel.'

He smiled and she waited for him to add that he didn't like cats, but he didn't.

She was all dizzy and confused by her insights because hadn't he told her last night that he got on with his dad?

She had talked about herself and really he'd told her nothing of him…

Was he just keeping things light?

Keeping it…just sex?

It felt more than that for her, though.

She needed to get away; she needed to think.

'I really ought to go,' Lina said again. She felt wooden. All the ease and the promise that had followed them into the bedroom had vanished.

'I'll drive you.'

'No, really...' She pulled on her clothes. 'I said I'd drop in on my mum while I'm over this way...' They both knew it was a lie, but out of politeness nothing further was said.

'Lina!'

Jeanette Edwards clearly wasn't expecting her daughter's company at eight on a Saturday morning, but thankfully the place was clear of whomever Lina's mother had done roots for and she was soon sitting at the kitchen table, nursing another coffee.

'What happened?' her mum asked.

'I met someone,' Lina attempted. 'Well, we've barely been out, but...' She tried her best to explain it. 'It feels like a whole lot more. I mean, it feels as if it could be something special.'

'Then what are you doing here?' Her mum laughed and then stopped herself. 'Sorry. Go on.'

Lina loved her mum, she truly did, and her mum was a wonderful person and great company.

If you were in a good mood.

Planet Jeanette, her dad had called it, often with a slight edge to his tone. It was a happy place, if slightly oblivious.

Lina's mum didn't like to talk about her daughter's work. 'It's a bit depressing really, isn't it?' she'd say, and find some chocolate biscuits, or a nice bottle of wine, or something funny on the Internet that she'd been dying to show her.

Her mum's answer to most problems was to simply cheer up and God alone knew that Lina wished she'd inherited at least some of that trait.

Her answer to Lina's being bullied at school had been, 'Stand up to them then.' Or, 'Stop being so sensitive.' Or, 'Well, I'll speak to your teacher...' which had brought Lina out in a cold sweat.

Really, Jeanette Edwards's level of TLC was the equivalent of Lina handing over her medic pack and the defibrillator and telling the patient they could take it from here.

Oh, and telling them they should come and watch this clip on YouTube once they were sorted.

Still, Lina badly needed some advice. 'Do you remember that patient who upset me a few years ago?'

'Sorry?'

'When I came here crying the morning after my shift...'

'Lina.' Mum blinked. 'From what I can remember, you were always crying after your shifts. That's why you left nursing.'

'No, not when I lived here, the one when I was in my grad year and there was that huge crash on the M25...'

'Not specifically, but then there have been a lot...'

'There was a woman, and she was pinned to the steering column and if we moved her—'

'Lina.' Jeanette stopped her then. 'I can't stand your stories. I'm sorry, I just...' She put up her hand and gave a little shake of her head. 'Did she die?'

'Yes!' That was the whole blessed point. Carrie had died and now six years later Lina was head over heels with her husband. 'She did die and—'

'I can't do this, Lina. I know you love your work, but, really, I don't need to hear about motorway crashes and things on a Saturday morning. I told you that. I can't take the drama of your job...'

The oddest thing was that Lina could remember a similar conversation, but between her dad and her mum, when he had come home worried about redundancies or something...

'You'll be fine.' Her mum had smiled to him.

She could clearly remember her dad's somewhat befuddled expression, because it was the same one that Lina was wearing now.

'So what about this fella?' her mum asked.

But instead of telling her, properly telling her, Lina made some vague comments and had four chocolate biscuits instead.

The journey back to her flat passed in a blur of jumbled thoughts.

'Whoo-hoo,' Shona said as Lina let herself into the flat, but then saw her pale face.

'Don't tell me…' Shona rolled her eyes. 'He's actually a visiting salesman with triplets…'

'Nothing like that,' Lina said, and she gave a tired smile.

'Then what's wrong?'

'I just…' She didn't know how to explain it, even if she'd wanted to. Lina settled for, 'It was a nice weekend. I just don't think we're particularly suited.' She gave a pale smile as she turned and headed off to her bedroom. 'Come here, Gretel,' she said, and lay with her friend purring on her chest. But it wasn't a new flatmate or the thought of finding a new place to live that consumed her; she would save all that for her walking trip.

Garth could not be cast aside until then.

Or rather Garth and Carrie.

The life he had once lived.

Did he ever find out that she had been pregnant? Lina wondered, and decided that he must have. And then her eyes filled up with tears, thinking of that.

Just that.

Garth alone and finding out he'd lost not just his wife but their baby too.

Might he blame her?

And later, an hour or so later, as she lay dry-eyed on her bed, a text pinged in from Garth.

It was a really nice text and she held her breath as she read how much he'd enjoyed their nights. It was flirty and sexy, and normally she'd be dancing around the room, but the perfect bubble had burst on them.

Then another text pinged in.

He'd really like to see her before she went on her trip, if that was okay.

She just stared at it for ages and guessed that this would be when he'd tell her about the life he'd once had…

How the hell was she supposed to tell him she already knew?

They either started on a lie or she ended it now…or she told him.

But how?

They'd been destined to end anyway, Lina told herself. She knew her own track record, and that was in a relationship without a dark past to deal with. How the hell could she have hope for this?

Her faith and skill in relationships were zero at best, but there was another dark niggle too, one she didn't want to examine.

Carrie had been stunning, all polished and elegant—even when she'd been dying!

That jazz-loving, wine-sipping, purple-dress-wearing woman that Garth had taken out on Friday night wasn't the real Lina.

She knew his likes and dislikes. In fact, she had the cheat sheet on him and was terrified she might use it.

And so, instead of sending a flirty message back, as she usually would, she sent him a thumbs-up emoji and then turned off her phone and cried.

They were over, Lina realised, before they'd even started.

CHAPTER EIGHT

BY MORNING LINA had rallied somewhat.

As she boiled the kettle in her freezing kitchen and made her sandwiches for work, Lina knew that she needed advice.

Male advice.

Certainly not from her brothers.

It had been Daniel's second wedding that she'd spoken about to Garth, and as for the other brother...well, suffice it to say she wouldn't go to either for relationship advice!

She was on morning shifts this week so Brendan would have to hold off on his phantom contractions for five minutes, Lina decided as she took her tear-streaked face to work.

And what did she get?

Kind, overly anxious Brendan and his endless patience? No, she got Perfect Peter who told her, 'Brendan's on paternity leave.'

'He didn't call me,' Lina frowned. 'What did Alison have?'

'She hasn't had it yet.' Peter rolled his eyes. 'In fact, they're not even at the hospital. It's probably another false alarm!'

And so she spent the day with Perfect Peter who, though less qualified and less experienced than her, thought he knew absolutely everything.

'Let's run through some scenarios,' he said as they waited for their next case.

Please, no, Lina thought, but didn't have the energy to debate so went along with it until thankfully her phone rang. It was Brendan, pacing the floor as, presumably, Alison did the same.

'The hospital said not to come in yet and that we should wait till the contractions were a bit closer, but honestly, Lina…'

'She's going to be fine.' Lina smiled and it was a genuine one, because there was extra space in a breaking heart and she was so excited for them. 'Enjoy every second, Brendan. Hold her hand, you're both going to be wonderful…'

Right when she needed to be busy, it was the longest, quietest day of her working life, interspersed with regular texts.

Two centimetres dilated!!

Lina smiled—it was certainly early days yet!

And then she didn't smile as Perfect Peter kept on with his scenarios.

Waiting for an epidural.

That was the text that arrived at midday. Finally back at home, Lina checked her texts and found that Alison had got to five centimetres...

Five centimetres!!!!! Alison is so amazing, she's on the phone to her mum!

And that evening as Lina sat with her grilled cheese on toast, which reminded her of Garth, the exclamation marks kept pace with Alison's cervix—by chance, she was sure, but she counted them anyway.

Eight centimetres!!!!!!!!

And then:

She's ready to push!

His excitement made Lina teary.

Brendan's love for his wife made her own love life feel so disastrous that she wanted to weep.

She should never have slept with Garth. They should have gone the old-fashioned route and held hands and got to know each other at a far slower pace and then he could have told her about Carrie in his own time.

Yet that didn't really help, because now, with her cheese toastie long since gone cold, there was a deeper reckoning to be had.

Garth didn't know her.

At least, not the real her.

She wasn't all polished and sophisticated, even if she'd tried to present herself as such on their date. Carrie had been the love of his life and it was hard for Lina to believe that she could ever hold a candle to that.

Her scars from every relationship she had ever attempted felt newly raw and exposed, and the honest truth was that, quite simply, she felt not good enough.

And then the text came that she'd been dreading all day.

Lina, is everything okay?

She stared at the phone. It wasn't Brendan; it was Garth.

She replied that everything was fine, and said she was just busy at work and she was on her way to a job so had to go.

And at midnight, freezing cold and so sad, she crawled into bed. Her phone bleeped again.

Somehow, she knew it wouldn't be Garth.

She had frozen him out enough.

It was happy news, though: Alison and Brendan had just had a healthy baby boy!

She did all the happy faces and emojis, even as tears streamed down her cheeks, and then she reached for Gretel and wept.

CHAPTER NINE

THE PRIMARY HOSPITAL was the very last place that Lina wanted to be.

Only that wasn't quite true.

She was so excited to see Brendan and Alison and their new baby, and a deeper truth was that, even if she was avoiding Garth, there was a painful conflict raging within her because she ached to see him.

In her lunch break she had bought the cutest little bodysuit and socks for the baby. As well as that she carried a floral arrangement with blue balloons and even an ambulance balloon, from all the guys and gals back at base.

She felt like a fugitive, dashing past Emergency with her head down and hopefully hidden by the flowers and balloons. She was just breathing a sigh of relief when she made it to the elevators, only to see Garth stepping out of the one she was going into.

'Lina.' He said it almost wearily.

'Garth!' She jumped at the delicious sight of him and her senses shot into overdrive as she did her level best to appear calm.

He was wearing navy trousers, a white shirt and a dark tie and had pagers clipped to his pockets but was looking very polished and smart.

And Lina, who didn't usually blush, could feel herself going bright red. She hoped it could be blamed on the heat of the hospital and on the fact that she was wearing a scarf and coat. 'I was just on my way to—'

'Maternity!' Garth stated the obvious on her behalf as he glanced at the large cloud of balloons and flowers she held.

'Yes.'

'So your partner had his baby?'

'Well, Alison did all the work but, yes, they just had a little boy. Yesterday,' she added.

'That's nice.'

'Very.'

He waited—not even a second, but it felt like if not a minute passed then certainly he left enough of a gap for her to explain why she hadn't returned his call, or to say that perhaps they could catch up again. Or...

She stood there awkward and silent.

'I should let you get on,' Garth said.

'Thanks,' Lina said, and hurried into the lift. 'It was nice seeing you.'

He gave her a slightly wide-eyed look that told him they both knew she'd lied.

Except, as the lift doors closed, Lina knew it wasn't a lie—it was so nice to have seen him.

And so painful too.

She wanted to press the ground floor button and plunge down and dash after him, and say…

What?

Suggest they go to the canteen and somehow tell him what she had remembered? But how?

The guy was trying to move on with his life and Lina had pegged herself as a transition gal at best.

Visiting hours for Maternity had commenced, and she was guided down the corridor towards a single-bed room where she knocked on the open door.

'Lina!' Alison was sitting up in bed and wearing a big smile, as Brendan paced with their baby.

'Congratulations!' Lina gave her a kiss and handed over the present and balloons and flowers. 'How are you?'

'So happy,' Alison said. 'Everyone has been so nice. I'm so tired, though.'

'I won't stay long.'

'Don't be daft.' Alison smiled.

'Can I peek?'

'Go ahead,' Brendan said. 'You can even hold him.'

'Oh, my goodness,' she said as she took the tiny, perfect bundle of love. He was all fat and chunky with blond sticking-up hair and he was absolutely so gorgeous that she thought she might cry. 'He looks like you!' she said to Brendan. 'Well, he's got more hair.'

'A mini-me.'

'I want one,' Lina admitted.

'Well, this one's taken.' Brendan smiled. 'Hey, did you know Richard's wife is a midwife here?'

Richard was one of the ED consultants. 'No.'

'Well, she is and she delivered him.'

And then they went into all the details that new parents did, but Lina didn't mind a bit because she was holding the warm bundle of baby. She gazed at his little red face as Alison told her that they were going to get him christened soon.

Very soon.

In fact, the weekend after she got back from her trip.

'We're waiting for you...' Brendan said.

'Thank you.'

Alison spoke then. 'We want you to be his godmother, Lina.'

It was the nicest surprise, just the absolutely nicest surprise, and it was soon followed by another, because when she stepped out of the elevator Garth was waiting for her.

Lina honestly hadn't been expecting that.

Usually guys seemed to melt away, right around the very second that Lina started liking them. Not this one, though. He was leaning against the wall, but stood up straight as she got out of the lift.

'Hey,' Garth said.

'Hey.'

'How was the visit?'

'Really nice,' she said. 'They've called the baby Michael. He's very cute.'

They walked together down the long corridor and the silence between them was strained. It was broken by Garth. 'Your self-help book was right.'

'Really?' Despite trying to play it cool, she could not hide her curiosity and turned and smiled. 'Did you finish all of your paperwork, then?'

'Better,' Garth said. 'I got started on the unpacking and it's finally done. Well, almost, but I've been putting it off for ages.' He took a breath. 'I don't like how we left things, Lina.'

'Sorry?' She attempted to sound as if she had no idea what he was referring to, despite it having been excruciating and never off her mind ever since.

'You're making me feel like a stalker.'

'What do you mean?'

'What do you *think* I mean? You're avoiding me.'

They were outside Emergency.

'No, of course I'm not.'

'Yes,' Garth said. 'Absolutely you are. You jumped out of your skin when you saw me beside the lift.'

'I didn't.'

'Yes, Lina, you did,' Garth said. 'You sent a thumbs-up emoji when I texted that I'd enjoyed our day in bed.'

'I'm sorry.' She blew out a breath. He would never understand how much thought had gone into that, even if it didn't translate as such. 'Look, it was lovely and everything...' She tried to end it in the same way so many had with her.

'But now it isn't?' Garth checked.

'Yes,' Lina admitted, because that at least was true. The simplicity of their desire for each other had turned into something very complicated, and she truly didn't know what to do for the best.

She didn't know how to, or even if she should, tell him.

She looked at his gorgeous face, and his navy eyes were searching hers.

She was tempted to suggest they go for Greek, his favourite—or should she say Italian to put him off?

She wanted to return to their simple world of toasted sandwiches and almond croissants and never have remembered the truth.

'I don't like jazz.'

'Excuse me?'

'I just don't think we'd work.'

'Because you don't like jazz?' He looked at her incredulously. He clearly thought he had her pegged as he said next, 'It was just sex you wanted?'

'Yep.'

Unlike most men she knew, he didn't smile and suggest a repeat. Instead, he fixed her with his eyes and responded tartly, 'Well, I'm glad to have satisfied.' And then his lovely face got back to the grumpy one she'd first met, and the nicest guy she'd ever been with turned and stalked off.

She was tempted to run after him, to tell him she was doing this for him and trying not to break his heart twice.

Except that wasn't strictly true.

Lina was terrified of baring her soul, of sharing what she knew just to have him ultimately walk away. But even so, it was eating her up, and it made her feel wretched.

Brendan was right: she went into things expecting to be let down. No, Garth was nothing like her dad. He was solid and dependable, she could feel it in her bones. But she was so exhausted trying to navigate this world on instinct alone, and had read men wrong so very many times.

She needed advice, but from whom?

Brendan was floating on the pink cloud of parenthood. She thought of May, but then immediately discounted that idea. After all, May worked with Garth.

For better or worse, Lina found herself back at her mum's.

'When does the baby come home?' her mum asked as she filled the kettle.

'Tomorrow,' Lina said. 'Brendan's coming back to work for a couple of weeks while Alison's mum's staying there, then he's going to take a full month off.'

'More than your father did.'

Lina took a breath and decided it was safer to just let that one go. 'I've been asked to be godmother,' Lina said as her mum plonked a cup of coffee down in front of her.

'That's nice.'

'Mum,' Lina said, 'you know that guy I was telling you about…' She looked at her mum and faltered. She didn't know how to give her the whole picture without including the sad part, so she told her the difficult part instead. 'The thing is, I've applied for a position in Newcastle.'

'Newcastle?'

'Yes,' Lina said.

'Why on earth would you want to move away, Lina? You love London. Your family's here…'

'I know all that, but I can't afford my own place. Maybe if I moved in here for a few months and saved like crazy…' Even as she said it Lina knew it was the most ridiculous idea.

Her mum agreed! 'Lina, I had three children by the time I was your age and I wasn't asking to move home every time the going got tough.'

'I know.'

'And what's all this got to do with this man you like?'

'Nothing,' Lina admitted. 'Nothing,' she said in a more resolute voice. After all, if she couldn't make a relationship work from the other side of London, what hope was there from the other side of the country?

She was scared, scared to stop and admit just how much she liked him, only to be served another lecture on how men always let you down in the end.

And there was something else, something she hadn't told her mum, let alone admitted it to herself.

Garth Hughes was, she was certain, completely out of her league.

It wasn't about pasta or cats, or jazz, it was about Lina, who would surely be a letdown when he got to know the real her, so she looked at her mum and simply said, 'I think it's time for a fresh start.'

CHAPTER TEN

BREAK-UPS HAD HURT her ego in the past, but this one hurt at a level she'd never known before.

It actually hurt her heart.

It was as if there was a knot in her chest and her lungs could not quite fill. Her shifts couldn't end soon enough and work wasn't exactly brilliant either.

She was invited to attend an interview in Newcastle, and given it was on the way to the Scottish borders, she arranged it for Friday morning and juggled around her reservations and train tickets.

She even made an appointment to view a couple of flats and a house.

Perfect Peter was his usual annoying self, insisting they go through scenarios during their down time, and actively questioning her choice as to whether to call in advanced practitioners in front of a patient's family at one point.

Lina, who had learnt to be forthright and stand up for herself, found that she struggled to do so in this case.

'Don't ever do that again,' she said once the patient was in the care of advanced practitioners and was being blue lighted to the nearest emergency department.

'Do what?'

'Speak down to me in front of a patient. It does nothing for their confidence.'

'I wasn't questioning you...'

'Well, it sounded like it.'

'I was questioning myself,' Peter said. 'He didn't quite fit the protocol.'

She looked over and saw his tense features. She thought of Huba and the way Garth had supported her by shadowing her for a few days... Gosh, why did all roads in her mind lead to him?

'I know that,' she said, 'but by the time they got there he did.'

'Yes, but...' He took a breath. 'I'd wanted to call them earlier...'

Lina blinked in surprise She'd actually thought he'd been opposing her calling for assistance.

'I was trying to remind myself to stick

with the protocols. I just struggle with acute asthmatics, *okay*?'

His *okay* was curt, a warning to end the conversation, but she looked at her colleague and knew now that his abruptness might be less about his colleagues and more about his own demons.

'Look,' Lina said, 'why don't we run through it together when we get back to base?'

He nodded.

'And,' she added, 'for what it's worth, I found that patient really tough. It's not always black and white. Yes, we called for back-up a bit early, but it turns out we were right to do so.'

They got on a bit better after that. The days ticked by and life carried on—except she didn't like the world as much as she had when Garth had been in her orbit.

Not even Brendan's return, on her final night before her break, brought back her easy smile, though she tried. 'What happened?' he asked in a lull between patients.

'Nothing.'

'What's going on?'

'Too much time working with Peter,' Lina said, hoping that would end the questioning.

'You can handle Peter, Lina,' Brendan said. 'Is it the jazz guy?'

'Leave it.'

'Who ended it?'

'Nobody ended it,' Lina said. 'We barely even got started. I don't like jazz and he hates cats.' Usually this would be enough said, but still Brendan stared. 'It just didn't work out, *okay*?' She used the same 'okay' that Peter had, the same 'okay' that said, *Leave well alone...this hurts too much to discuss*.

Except Brendan seemed not to hear it and asked, 'So why are you still moping about?'

'I'm not moping,' Lina snapped. She was still trying to recover from the loss of all she had felt for him and there wasn't a person in the world she could tell who might understand that she felt as if she'd touched love. 'Can you just leave it, Brendan, please?'

He didn't answer, just munched on his orange segments.

'How's Michael doing?' she asked, hoping to change the subject.

'He's got reflux,' Brendan said, 'so we're trying him on this new formula. God, I used to think I'd be calm. I mean, we've seen the lot, but it just changes things, Lina.'

'I know.'

'But you don't know.'

This annoyed her. Just because she didn't

have a baby, she couldn't possibly know what it meant, and so she sulked and looked out of the window.

'What's really going on?' Brendan asked.

'Nothing,' Lina answered sarcastically. 'And even if there were, how could I possibly know, given I've never had a real relationship?'

'All right, my five days of fatherhood doesn't make me an expert on being a parent, but I know what I'm talking about when it comes to relationships.'

'Leave it, Brendan,' she warned.

'Nope,' he said. 'I won't.'

'You've had one serious relationship.'

'And that number has stayed at one because we both work at it,' Brendan responded, and that made Lina catch her breath because he and Alison really did work at it. They fought for their relationship, but she didn't know how to do that.

'Please, Brendan,' she asked, 'can you just let it go?'

Thankfully, he had no choice but to leave it as they were called to a job. Unfortunately, it was one of the patients that got to Lina the most.

Not a patient who was desperately ill, or

a situation involving high drama, just a person who really deserved better.

William Carter, known as Bill, aged eighty-six, had been on the floor for some time.

Lina didn't know why it was these patients that upset her the most, just that they did.

'Hello, Bill,' she said as she looked around his tiny flat. She saw the large chair that he'd fallen out of and the spot on the floor where he had lain for several hours after inching across the floor enough to reach his phone.

'I'm frozen,' he said, 'and I haven't fed Blinky.' As Brendan started to look him over, Lina went and found a large blanket to cover him with and turned on the small heater too.

They did a thorough examination, although Bill kept insisting there was nothing broken except his pride. 'Just get me back into the chair.'

'Is that where you sleep?' Lina checked.

'Yes.' Bill nodded. 'It's easier than getting in and out of bed.'

'Do you have anyone come in and help you?'

'Sandra, my daughter, comes in a couple of times through the week, and drops off my shopping and things. She does my washing too. She wants to do more, but she's got MS...'

'What about carers?' Lina pushed for more information.

'I don't need any of that,' Bill huffed. 'I just need you to get me back into my chair. I don't want strangers in my home when I can manage fine by myself.'

He clearly wasn't managing.

And tonight neither was she, but she blew out a breath and pushed back the threat of tears. 'We just need to check your heart before we move you,' Lina said, but that wasn't what Bill wanted.

'I want to get back in my chair and have a cup of tea,'

But a cup of tea wasn't going to fix this.

'Bill, we really do need to take you in,' Lina said as she looked at the monitor. 'Your heart isn't behaving.'

'If you'd just fetch me my blood pressure tablets...'

'Bill,' she said, looking at the hopeless surroundings and this proud old man trying to battle on.

'Why don't you let us take you to hospital for a check-up?' Brendan took over then, trying to persuade him to go to hospital, but

Bill was having none of it and insisted he would be fine here.

'I just need a tea and a couple more of my tablets.' He thumped the floor in frustration and Lina could see angry tears filling his eyes. 'And if you can feed Blinky, then I'll be fine.'

Blinky was a budgerigar who was chirping away under a sheet. Lina found herself in the little kitchenette attached to the lounge, searching under the sink, while Bill shouted instructions. Finally, she located the bird seed and as she did, she paused, took a little breath, and closed her eyes.

'You okay?' Brendan checked as he came over to fill the kettle and give Bill his tea.

Yes, she was about to say, *I'm fine*.

Like Bill, just soldier on and pretend things weren't falling apart.

Perhaps that was why patients like Bill got to her so much—they were too used to going it alone.

She thought of May, offering to talk, and Brendan extending the hand of friendship, but like Bill she'd refused.

She was tired of being too tough and too scared to reveal herself, but tears were so close that she had no choice. 'I'm not great,' she admitted bravely. Out of the corner of her mouth she told him the truth. 'It is the jazz guy… Garth Hughes.'

Brendan shook his head. Clearly Garth Hughes wasn't the centre of his world, or even in his orbit.

She'd hid it so well.

'The consultant at The Primary.'

'The miserable one,' Brendan said, dunking the tea bag. 'You really know how to pick them. We'll talk later.'

'Thanks.' Lina nodded.

'I won't forget.'

They headed out to deal with Bill and the tough old Lina was finally back, even if she was holding a box of birdseed! 'Bill.' Lina was firmer this time. 'Your blood pressure is dangerously high, your tablets haven't brought it down, and neither has the patch. What if you hadn't been able to reach your phone?' She told him the bitter truth. 'You could have had a stroke.'

'I'd have been fine,' he insisted.

'When is Sandra coming in again?' She asked.

'Monday.'

'So on Monday Sandra would have found you.' She watched as he closed his eyes, despondent at the thought of his daughter finding him on the floor, no doubt in a worse condition than this.

'She'd have called before then and if she'd got no answer...' His voice trailed off and then he admitted some of what was on his mind. 'But what about Blinky?'

'I'm going to feed Blinky and then Brendan and I are going to take you to hospital. Bill, you need your medication to be reviewed,' Lina said, 'and hopefully the hospital can sort some proper home help and support for you...' She looked at the undressed ulcers on his leg. 'There's so much more that can be done for you, but you have to let us help.' He wasn't arguing now, Lina noted. 'Brendan and I can't do it all from this end. We can call your GP, but, really, you're not well enough to leave on your own tonight.'

'Fair enough...' Bill mumbled. 'Careful when you—' But he was too late. The cage door opened and Blinky took his chance and flew out. Even Bill joined in laughing as he watched Brendan's attempts to catch him.

Blinky sat on the curtain rail, surveying them all. In the end, Bill whistled and the little blue bird flew onto his shoulder. 'Why didn't you do that in the first place?'

Lina smiled as she returned the escapee to his cage.

'He needs his exercise before I go,' Bill said. 'I might be gone a few days.'

'You'll be back soon enough,' Lina said, glad that Bill had accepted he needed some proper help.

'Should I put the cover back over him?' Brendan asked.

'I don't know,' Bill admitted. 'Sandra might not get here till Monday...'

They both looked at Brendan, who was clearly to be the budgerigar expert. 'Well, it might not be fair to leave him in the dark till then.'

'Why don't we leave the radio on for him?' Lina suggested, so the radio went on and Bill said goodnight to Blinky. She had the craziest job in the world at times!

'Am I going to Barnet?' Bill asked as they got him settled into the back of the ambulance. It was Brendan's turn to drive and Lina sat with Bill while Brendan waited for instructions.

'Let's find out.'

It was a busy night this side of town, though, and Brendan gave her a knowing look when they were cleared to take Bill to The Primary. 'Your favourite place.'

Not.

She was like a cat burglar every time they ended up there, but thankfully, so far, Lina had avoided seeing Garth again.

'Well, this is nice.' May greeted them all with a smile.

'I thought you'd finished with nights,' Lina said, surprised to see that May was on duty.

'So did I! So what have you got for me?'

'William Carter,' Lina started, but Bill butted in before she had a chance.

'Bill,' he said. 'And I'm hoping for some tea before you leave me to wait.'

'Well, lucky for you we're not too busy to-night.' May smiled and guided them straight to a cubicle.

'You're lucky we're not here with a bird in tow,' Brendan quipped.

'Oh, I've had worse,' May said, and she clucked around Bill and chatted to him as she always did, but managed a quick word over her shoulder to Lina. 'Can I have a word before you go?'

As Brendan changed the blankets, May and Lina stood in the corridor, waiting. 'I did that reference.'

'Thanks.' Lina pushed out a smile. 'I'm

heading up there in the morning and then I've got an interview the next day...'

'You're taking the train?'

'As soon as I finish my shift. I had to fiddle around with the bookings for my trip, but it worked out really well.' She could see Garth at the nurses' station and he glanced over; Lina quickly looked away. 'I really do have to go, but thanks so much, May.'

Lina sat in the bright foyer on the jump seat. For once she just let Brendan do all the work to restock the ambulance while she just sat there, wondering what to do.

'He was looking right at you,' Brendan said. 'That Garth.'

'I know,' Lina said.

'So what happened?'

'Not here.'

'Yes, here,' Brendan said, 'or something will come up and we'll get called to a job and before we know it morning will be here and you'll be on your trip.'

And looking at houses and being interviewed for a job she wasn't sure that she wanted.

'It was just a short-term thing...' Lina attempted, as that was what she kept telling herself, but this time her eyes filled with tears. 'It just felt like more at the time.'

Could you glimpse for ever in a single weekend? Was there really such a thing as love?

'I've never seen you like this, Lina. I've never seen you cry...'

'He's a widower,' Lina gulped.

'He's not over his wife?' Brendan asked, trying to hazard a guess as to what had gone wrong.

'No,' she interrupted, 'I don't know. He hasn't even told me he's a widower yet.'

'So how do you know?'

Before she launched into the story, she said, 'You can't tell anyone...'

'I'll tell Alison.'

And that made her cry even harder, and made her trust him even more. So she told Brendan that she'd realised that she'd cared for Garth's wife when she'd been dying, because she trusted him as both a colleague and a friend—and the nicest thing about Brendan was that tears filled his eyes as she explained what had happened.

'How long ago did she die?'

'I was a grad—so nearly six years now. You'd never really get over it, though...'

'I wouldn't,' Brendan said. 'I'd be a miserable old git without Alison.'

'He is…' Lina smiled '…but then suddenly he isn't…' She couldn't quite explain, and neither would she try to articulate the reward of his smile and the pure happiness they'd glimpsed together.

How he hadn't cared that she'd turned purple—and neither had she.

How she'd told Garth about her dad and how she missed him, when she'd never told that to another soul.

'When did you realise that you'd looked after his wife?' Brendan asked.

'He seemed familiar but I couldn't put my finger on it. And then…' She didn't want to admit that it was just after they'd made love, as that seemed too personal. 'Maybe I should have recognised him sooner, but—'

'Lina,' Brendan interrupted, 'we get called to so many accidents, and there are so many patients, we'd go crazy if we remembered the details of each and every one.'

'I do remember the details of this one now, though. Should I tell him?' Lina said. 'I mean, would you want to be told?'

'I don't know,' Brendan admitted. 'If it's just a short-term thing, probably not, but if…' He blew out a breath and pictured Alison rather than Carrie. 'I actually don't know what to say here, Lina.'

'Some expert.' She gave him a watery smile. 'I know too much about him. And talking about it is going to really hurt him. I think he was working up to tell me he was a widower and he was already struggling enough with that…'

'You have to have the difficult conversations, Lina.'

'And hurt him in the process?'

'Sounds like you're managing to do that already.' He gave her a tissue and she wiped her eyes. 'You do know how to pick them,' Brendan said, and she laughed grudgingly.

'Thanks for listening,' Lina said.

But Brendan wasn't content with just listening. 'I think you need to talk to him. He knows you're avoiding him.'

'Yes, he does!'

They both jumped at the sound of Garth's voice.

Lina froze.

'Are you going to tell me why?'

Brendan offered to make himself scarce. 'I might go and try to find a coffee before we clear. Do you want one, Lina?'

'Please.'

As Brendan headed off, Garth climbed

into the ambulance and stood in front of her. One of the things she really liked about Garth was that he was direct. 'Did we take it too fast?'

'No.' If only it was as simple as that.

And then in the midst of her misery he made her smile with his next question. 'Am I dreadful in bed?'

She let out a short, watery laugh but her eyes filled with tears. 'You know you're not.' In his arms, life had been as close to perfect as she had ever known.

And clearly he had felt that way too, because he was here, trying to work out what had gone wrong. 'Well, between that and waking up, something happened, Lina.'

After days of mulling it over, and finally telling Brendan everything, she still didn't know what to say.

'I'm pretty good at reading people,' Garth continued, 'and knowing when things are going wrong. God knows, I've had practice. But one moment we seemed fine—better than fine—and I know I haven't felt like that in a long time. Not since...' Lina looked down at her boots. She couldn't meet his eyes as he spoke on. 'I haven't been completely upfront with you, Lina. I was married...' He must have seen her pale face and assumed she was thinking the worst—that he was in the middle of a torrid divorce or had ten children or something… 'I'm widowed.'

'I'm sorry.'

She felt a little bit sick, along with that guilty feeling that made you swallow.

'I didn't tell you at the time,' Garth continued, 'but I was about to. I wanted to get unpacking the flat out of the way first…' She sat there, saying nothing. 'There's no logic in that, I guess, but I've been struggling with where to put things…' His voice trailed off.

'I get it,' Lina said, and then thought about her words with Brendan. 'Well, inasmuch as I can…'

'Maybe we did take things a bit fast,' Garth went on. 'Maybe I should have told you sooner, but it tends to put a dampener on things and also…it's not something I talk about easily.'

'I understand,' Lina said.

She did.

Life and love weren't like a medical handover.

You shouldn't have to introduce yourself as the widower who had lost the absolute love of your life, straight off the bat.

Or the not girly enough dating disaster...
They had been at the beginning of all that,
yet in other ways they had been so much
closer than that... But actually, understanding his explanation as she was reminded of
the mountain of boxes in the bare flat, and
how hellish it must be to shed little pieces
of yourself with each move.

'I always knew the second I'd upset her,
though,' Garth said. 'And in all failed attempts at relationships since, well, I can pin-
point the second it goes wrong—although
it's usually about fifteen minutes in...'

'Because they weren't her?'

'Yep,' he admitted. 'But I've worked on
myself and I got past that, and then along
came you, but for the life of me I just can't
figure out where it all went wrong. I mean,
I know now you're not into jazz, and maybe
it wasn't a great venue for a first date, but
we were fine afterwards...'

'It wasn't that.' She felt a hot tear trickle
down her cheek. 'It wasn't your fault.'

'Please don't tell me it's not me, it's you...'

She smiled. 'It's us.'

'I don't get it.'

'I remembered something, Garth.' Her
voice was strained because even that rel-
egated what had happened to him—the

most life-changing, devastating, event of his life—to no more than a difficult shift for her. 'The first night we met,' she said, 'I walked into the staffroom and you were asleep in the chair.' Garth frowned; clearly he had no idea where this was going, and that, of course, was the issue. 'I felt as if I'd seen you before. Then later I put it down to having bumped into you at work or something.'

He was very quiet.

'Then after we…' Now it was Lina who fell quiet for a second, remembering the bliss of his bed and the joy they had found before reality had invaded. 'I realised… I remembered…'

She took a deep breath. It was now or never.

'Garth, I was working on the night of your accident…'

'Sorry?' He frowned and for a wild second Lina dreamt that she was mistaken, that she had mixed him up…but of course it was just hope clouding her senses, for she actually watched the colour leach from his face. She watched the thwack to his head as she sent him back into hell, the same hell he must have fought to claw his way out of. 'Were you working in Emergency?'

'No.' Lina shook her head. 'As a paramedic.'

'You saw…' His voice was croaky. 'I was unconscious the whole time. I don't remember… Did you take care of me?'

'No.' She shook her head and said the hardest part. 'I took care of Carrie.'

He sat down on the stretcher and she watched this big bear of a man put his head in his hands and drag in deep breaths.

She was crying but silently. Perhaps it wasn't even her place to cry here, but she couldn't stop tears from falling.

'You were with her?' Garth checked.

Lina nodded. 'Well, I was part of a team but, yes, I was with her.'

'I know that she was conscious for a while…' He swallowed. 'Did she speak to you?'

'Yes.' Lina nodded. 'She spoke about you and…' she swallowed '…her family and childhood, and…' She finally looked right at him. 'You. She spoke a lot about you.' He didn't look up and she didn't know how to fill the silence, but she had to go on. 'I didn't know how to tell you, or even whether I should.' She had been privy to details not by choice but by the nature of her work. 'She told me things…'

'Things?'

'Big things…like about your honeymoon. And little things too—you don't like coffee…' Her voice trailed off. 'I am so sorry.'

'You have nothing to be sorry for.' He said it, except it sounded more like an automatic response than a heartfelt one. Just a stab at politeness as he negated what she'd revealed.

'No.'

It just sucked.

'I don't know what to say here, Lina.'

'Neither do I.'

He looked up then and she could see the agony in his eyes.

Did Garth even know that she'd been pregnant? He must because it would have been in the coroner's report, yet it was another thing a new girlfriend should not yet know.

'It messed with my head,' Lina admitted. 'I'm not very good at relationships. I always seem to get things wrong, or say the wrong thing…'

'By telling me about Carrie?' He frowned. His face was so pale. She guessed that he was still reacting to the fact that they were in a cold, bright ambulance talking about his late wife's death, and so she attempted to pull on her professional hat. 'If there's anything you want to ask, about Carrie, I mean, about that night…'

He stared back for the longest time before speaking. 'I'm sure I should have some questions. And of course I do. It's just…'

'A shock?' Lina ventured.

'Yes. Of all the things I thought had gone wrong between us, I never thought it might be that…'

'No.'

Neither really knew what to say. There were questions that might or might not need answers, and there was more trouble that a couple at the very beginning of a relationship should have to face.

His past sat between them, and it would seem that neither knew how to deal with that.

'I ought to get back in,' he said. 'May's going to be wondering where the hell I've got to.'

It sounded like a normal conversation except his skin was the colour of putty and for the first time ever he was completely unable to meet her eyes.

Lina too was brilliant at noticing the very second things went wrong, because as he stood up and gave her a thin smile, Lina knew that it would be Garth avoiding her now.

'Garth?' She called him back, but for a second it looked as if he was going to keep right on walking, but just as he reached the doors, instead of stepping down, he halted and slowly turned around.

'I wanted to tell you.'

'But you didn't.'

They were the three hardest words that Lina had ever heard and they were laced with accusations that she didn't want to interpret. It seemed he was taking back his earlier words and that she did have something to be sorry about. 'You could have told me in bed. You could have called. You could have done it so much better than you did. I'm at work...' And that made her breath hitch in her throat as he put up his hands. 'I can't deal with this now. I've got a department full of patients and a night shift to complete...'

He was angry.

Not with her.

Yes, with her.

And he was embarrassed as he made his way back to the department.

Embarrassed because he didn't want anyone to have seen him like that, soiled and bleeding and helpless, as the woman he'd loved had lain dying by his side.

It was private.

'Garth?' May called to him. 'Can I get you to cast your eyes over—?'

'Get Huba,' he snapped.

Yes, he was angry. Huba was fine now, her confidence restored, while he was back to where he'd started—or rather back to where his life had ended and in that dark pit of grief.

'Garth?' May found him standing in his office. 'What on earth…?'

And May, who for six months had been needling him for information and getting nothing, didn't even try to find out what was wrong, because she knew agony when she saw it, and his was pure.

She was watching him drowning.

'Can you call Richard and ask him to come in and cover…?' Garth said in a voice that was struggling to form words, coming from lungs that had forgotten how to breathe.

'Of course,' May said. 'I'll do it right now.'

'And if Huba needs me, I'll come round but—'

'She's fine,' May said as Garth looked around blindly for a chair as if he had no idea where it might be located. 'You did too good a job with her. She's a bit arrogant now really.' May nattered on as she guided him to the said foreign object and somehow he managed a small smile at her words and then sat there, numb. Not once did May ask him why, or what was wrong,

She just accepted that it was.

Completely wrong.

The same way the world had been wrong when he'd started coming to and found himself in hospital, his father, who he didn't get on with, sitting by his bed.

And still sitting there that evening when he'd briefly opened his eyes.

His father had still been there the next morning as he'd flitted back to the world.

Garth had known, therefore, that Carrie was dead before he'd been told.

Now May made him tea, and he stared at the muddy brown liquid. Even a cup of tea was more complicated now, because he was remembering that morning, the very second he had pegged that the Lina he had gone to bed with wasn't the same Lina that had woken up beside him…

He sat in his office, hoping no serious cases came in, and then nodded in weak relief when May told him that Richard had arrived, but then added that there was no way he was driving home.

'I can walk it,' he told her.

'Not yet you can't.'

May was right.

And so he sat there some more.

CHAPTER ELEVEN

THE NIGHT DRAGGED on and on. And, no, he didn't call.

And Lina, who was more than used to checking her phone for guys who didn't call, this time found that the lack of contact made her feel ill.

His silence was agony.

Her handling of the whole thing had her spinning as she packed for her trip and she wished she could take it back, wished she'd told him more gently. Sooner perhaps?

Why did he not just call?

Except in this case it was worse when he did.

As she stood at Euston Station, waiting to board her train, his name pinged onto her phone.

Thank you for telling me, Lina. If I came down

hard on you, I apologise. I know it must have been difficult.

She thought for a moment before responding.

It was.

Then she hit 'send' too soon and had to follow it up.

Though of course it was harder for you to hear it. I shouldn't have told you at work.

Another distinct lack of response, so once she had boarded the train and found her seat she fired another message.

Do you have any questions?

He didn't reply straight away. She could feel his strain even as the train pulled out of the station, and she was well out of London before her phone pinged. She was on the receiving end of a frown from a fellow passenger for daring to not silence her phone.

I don't think it's fair on either of us to ask them.

She looked at his text for a very long time before she finally answered.

You can.

There was no further response.

The plan had been to sleep on the train, but instead she just stared out at the English countryside and wished he was there beside her, that she could have wrapped her arms around him and made things right between them...

Made it hurt less.

But today everything hurt.

The sight of the bridges over the Tyne always moved her and the accents were familiar as she headed out of the station to find her accommodation.

There was a café she knew, and her aunt was nearby.

This place felt like home...

Almost.

Everything was making her cry today, so much so that she had to duck out of her little bed & breakfast and buy an eye mask in the hope of looking normal for her interview the next day.

Oh, that.

Lina was torn, so torn.

It was a massive decision she was about to make. It was stay or go and it deserved her full attention—except she couldn't focus on that because it was a future without Garth that was killing her now.

She'd feel better in the morning, Lina told herself as she ate a sandwich she'd bought on the train and told herself to get some sleep. But Garth was on her mind the whole night through. So much so that she deliberately switched off 'Do Not Disturb' on her phone and kept leaping in hope every time it bleeped, only to find it was *just* the news—or rather not the news she was desperate for.

Garth.

She fell asleep with the agony of his features visible to her closed eyes, and the awful knowledge that she had caused it.

And she awoke to the same.

Interview day dawned and Lina was brilliant at putting on a brave face—it was an almost prerequisite for her job. Arm hanging off? Not a problem. Impaled on a fence? Nothing we haven't seen…

A shattered heart? Usually she could deal with that, except the diagnosis here was starting to look a whole lot like love, and these were uncharted waters for Lina.

She was tempted to be late for the interview, to sabotage all her chances, but somehow public transport decided to behave and she arrived with fifteen minutes to spare.

And they were all so welcoming.

'You were born here?'

'Yes.' Lina beamed, keeping her professional hat on and sounding upbeat. 'I spent most of my summers here. It's like a second home really…'

So why did her mind keep flicking to the four-in-the-morning feeling she got driving through London, and the laughter and camaraderie with her colleagues? Yes, even when she was paired with Perfect Peter. The many, many hospitals she attended, where everyone knew her by name, each one offering a different welcome but somehow never making her feel like the 'new girl'.

London, even if she couldn't afford it, even with all her issues, really was starting to feel like home.

Still, the interview went really well.

And the house viewing went even better.

There were two. One was a complete disaster, but there was one that she could actually afford. A two-bedroomed house with the steepest stairs ever, but the kitchen had been refurbished, and the bathroom was liveable, and there was a teeny garden out the back—not that Gretel would venture out.

But she could admire it from the window ledge.

Yes, it all went too well, because as she took the train from Newcastle up to the Scottish borders, a day later than initially planned, Lina knew that there could be no more putting things off and that choices had to be made.

The Borders were grey and sort of gothic, which perfectly matched her mood, and Lina loved it completely.

She booked into her little hotel and then wandered around the bitty shops and tried her level best to enjoy her getaway.

Bounce back, she told her heart. *Snap to it.*

She'd only spent one weekend with Garth, and by all accounts they were through, so he could have no bearing on the decision she was about to make.

Except, even with the lousy start it had been the best weekend of her life.

And breakfast at the café with Garth had been the best breakfast she'd known and she did not know how to explain to herself the pain of the absence of him in her life when he'd barely been in it.

It just felt as if he belonged there.

And even if they could never be, still she wanted to know how he was faring and to apologise for her handling of things, yet her phone remained stubbornly silent. And so she distracted herself by heading into a musty-smelling shop filled with old books and antiques, in her ongoing search for vintage ambulance models.

'We don't have any,' the man said. 'Pity you weren't here yesterday...'

'I was supposed to be,' Lina sighed, because that had been her initial plan before the interview had come up. He was carrying an armful of records that he was about to put on display, and once he had laid them out Lina found herself flicking through them.

There was a whole jazz collection section.

A whole world she'd never known!

'I'd buy that now if I were you,' the man said when he saw her looking at one. 'It will be snapped up.'

'Really?' Lina frowned.

It was, she was told by the man who turned out to be the owner, a piece of mint-condition vinyl by a famous jazz musician. She read the back and was sort of toying with it—after all, Garth had bought breakfast and dinner and she sort of wanted to close things on a better note. 'Is it for some-one?' the shop owner asked.

'Yes, though I think he likes modern jazz…' whatever the hell that was! 'I don't know if he's got anything to play it on.'

'He'd want this, believe me…'

He was either a completely brilliant sales-man or it would make the perfect gift—only Lina wasn't into sentimental gifts and any-way, they were over.

Except…

Perhaps she could send it to him, with a little note.

Or maybe a card?

Just to say that she had seen the vinyl and was thinking of him and hoped he was doing okay and that she was very sorry for her handling of things.

And *then* she could move on with her life…

Really move on.

It was a very expensive gift, as it turned out, and there was certainly no gift wrap-ping. He gave her an old paper bag and she carefully zipped it into her pack, and then she moved on to a coffee shop, which usu-ally helped to lift her mood. But it just didn't today.

She had a vanilla and malt milkshake *and* a chocolate éclair, but nothing helped.

Nothing helped.

Not even pizza delivered to her room because she was too teary and jumbled to go out. Instead she was sitting in her little B&B bedroom and crying her eyes out. If this was love, she didn't want it, because it simply hurt too much.

Oh, why didn't he call?

Why didn't Garth say they could put it behind them, and work on it?

He didn't.

But, then, Lina thought, neither had she.

She passed another lonely night, and in the morning it was misty and grey when she pulled back the curtains. The temptation to close the curtains and climb back into bed was unfamiliar and worrying. Not that she tended to bounce in the mornings, but she had never been so close to taking to her bed.

Instead, she hauled on her clothes and then stood in the tiny kitchen and hardboiled her eggs, and then made some sandwiches and a big flask of coffee, packed up her rucksack and checked out. The bus journey to St Abbs, which was to be the start of her planned walk, passed in a bit of a blur, but she was glad for the effort she'd made when she stepped off and walked down to the harbour. It was bracing and the air smelt of seaweed. The sky was grey, but the water was a deep, angry blue, while the fishing boats bobbed, and the lobster creels were all piled up at the sides.

She was glad to be here, Lina thought as she started the coastal walk.

She was through with men.

Only not quite.

Garth Hughes wasn't being added to the list of terrible mistakes. He had a heading of his own.

If Only.

Walking really was her de-stressor—the occasional good morning from a fellow human, a greeting from a dog, the wind in her face—this was how she sorted herself, Lina knew.

Concentrating on where she put her feet, or pausing to look at a magnificent view, it left her mind free to sort out the jumble of problems in the background, even if it dared not ponder the big one called Garth Hughes that seemed lodged in the foreground.

And later, sitting on a damp clump of heather, she knew that a decision had to be made—not about Garth as that felt too raw to deal with just yet. No, she had to make up her mind about moving and starting her life all over again.

She thought of the positives.

A tiny house of her own instead of sharing.

A patch of garden.

All these gorgeous walks a bus or train ride away.

A chance to advance her career.

She had some aunts and cousins nearby and she knew that paramedics were a friendly lot so her social life would be just fine.

Except…

She thought of little Michael, her soon-to-be godson, and Brendan and Alison and, yes, Shona, when she wasn't being a pain. And Mum and her brothers and May, who had offered to speak with her before she made such a decision.

Yes, she should have spoken to May about moving, because she wasn't just a colleague, she was a friend, a huge part of her world…

And then there was London.

Beautiful London that felt as if it was her own when the blue hour came just before dawn, and the best cafés she knew and the hospitals and her history and all the people she loved…

She couldn't avoid thinking about Garth and having to face him if she stayed. But as awkward as it might be, bumping into Garth on occasion—and it would be awkward, that much she knew—it wasn't a big enough reason for leaving.

Lina hadn't inherited her father's knack for running away.

The fact was that she loved London.

Even if she couldn't afford it.

Even if it meant having to see Marcus every morning as she hard-boiled her eggs and wearing earplugs every time he and Shona had sex until she'd saved enough for her own place…

One decision down, five thousand to go, Lina thought as she hauled herself up and rather gingerly made her way down a track so steep that she had to hold on to the handles.

Imagine falling here, Lina thought. Imagine having to retrieve a patient who had fallen here…

And then she nearly found out exactly how it would be done because her heart lurched and her legs almost gave way beneath her. Garth was on the beach, waiting for her.

She was surely seeing things.

Up ahead was a guy, a large guy with dark, wavy hair, watching her walk towards him.

It couldn't be him because she knew he was working this weekend and she was in Scotland, for goodness' sake…looking terrible.

So terrible!

She had on khaki trousers and a big raincoat and massive boots, and she was wet and red-faced, and certainly not profile-photo-ready! But it *was* Garth and he was walking towards her and looking a whole lot more together than her.

'I thought I might find you here,' Garth said, and then smiled at her bemused face. 'Well, I thought I might find you here yesterday…'

'I'm running a day behind schedule.'

'I know,' Garth said, 'because I was here yesterday too…'

'Why?'

'Waiting for you. In fact, I really am starting to feel like a stalker.'

'You're nothing of the sort.' Lina smiled.

She tried to keep her heart under control, and to stop herself from jumping into his arms and pleading for this purgatory to end, but then she reminded herself that Dr

Sensible probably had some things about Carrie that he wanted to ask and that was confirmed with what came next: 'I do have some questions I'd like to ask you, if that's okay.'

'Sure.' Lina nodded.

'It seemed wrong to ask them via text.'

'So you decided to rock up on my walk instead,' Lina teased, and was glad that he got her, because he smiled.

'Yes.'

There wasn't a lot of talking at first because they left the beach and found themselves on a fairly steep incline. Lina was glad of the silence just to get her head around the fact he was actually there.

And looking gorgeous, by the way!

His bum was fantastic and she sneaked a guilty look as she huffed her way behind and once, or maybe twice, she had to tell him to slow down. 'I'm not a walker walker...'

'That's right,' he said as he slowed down.

'I amble rather than ramble.'

So they ambled to the top and there she took a very long drink of water and then said, 'I am so sorry for telling you at work...'

'We'll get to that,' Garth said, like a schoolteacher temporarily filing away a misdemeanour.

For now they just walked, enjoying the bracing breeze and the seagulls swooping and calling, and the balm of nature.

'So this is what you do with your days off?'

'Pretty much.' Lina nodded. 'Well, not all of them, but it's my hobby, I guess. I came here as a little girl,' Lina said, smiling at the memory. 'Well, the next village over. I remember having ice cream and feeding a seal…'

'With your parents.'

'Yes,' Lina said.

'You miss him,' Garth said, not as a question, more an observation.

'Not right now,' Lina said. What she wanted to say was, *I miss you.*

He was here, but no doubt it was to find out more about his late wife.

Their walk was interspersed with benches carrying plaques in memory of people who must have loved to sit and take in the stunning views too.

'Do you want to sit?' Garth suggested, and she nodded.

They were both shy and nervous, and though they knew this difficult conversation had to be had, they didn't dive straight in. 'I've got lunch,' Lina said as she opened up her rucksack, 'if you want to share it.'

'Sounds good.'

Egg sandwiches had never tasted so good, but he declined her coffee and stuck with his water, and they just sat, enjoying the feel of the wind whipping their hair and cheeks and the majesty of the rugged North Sea.

'How was your interview?' Garth asked.

She turned and her mouth gaped. Not the best look mid-sandwich, so she rapidly closed it and swallowed before croaking, 'How do you know about that?'

'I heard May giving you a reference, just before we went out...'

'Ouch.' Lina cringed. Maybe that was the reason that the mood might have been a bit flat at first.

'So, how did it go?'

'Brilliantly,' Lina replied. 'Too brilliant,' she then sighed. 'I didn't know how to tell you about it. I mean, I would be the stalker if I told you on our first date that I was thinking of dropping my plans to move away on the back of one breakfast, one night out...'

'Probably,' he said, 'but, then, with the way we were that weekend, probably not.'

'I need to give Shona an answer.'

'Why don't you text her and say yes, it

would be great if Marcus moved in, because Garth wants to move in too?' He smiled as she laughed and he didn't need to tell her he was joking. It was funny to picture Shona's face if she did, but way better than that was the return of his smile.

'I'm staying,' Lina said. 'I'm happy at work, I've got brilliant friends, and I'm sure, well, I'm determined to find somewhere that is affordable just for me, hopefully with a little balcony...' she thought for a daunting moment '...that doesn't mind a cat.'

'How's Gretel?' Garth asked as they shared a bag of crisps.

'Temperamental,' she said. 'But Shona is looking after her and I've bought her some extra treats to have while I'm away.'

'That's good.'

She turned and faced him, feeling a little braver now. 'I know you hate cats...' He looked at her and frowned. 'Carrie told me you did.'

'Really?' He blinked in surprise and then he smiled; she guessed he was replaying memories with his late wife. 'I don't hate cats, I just told Carrie that I did...'

She swallowed as he said her name.

'The thing was that her parents had this

cat, Suky. Honestly, Lina, this cat had a face
that could haunt houses. She was the scari-
est thing you've ever seen, and they were all
over her... I just blanched when I saw her
and then to cover said that I just don't like
cats. However, that's not strictly true. I'm
sure Gretel's beautiful.'

'She is.' Lina smiled and looked at him,
and suddenly it wasn't so terrible because he
had said her name, and told a little of his history, and they were still standing—or rather
sitting—smiling at each other.

'I was going to tell you about her,' Garth
said. 'When I went in to do all the paperwork, I was determined to do it that night,
but then you threw a picnic in my lounge
with Christmas pudding and everything, and
the time just didn't seem right.'

'That's why you haven't had Christmas
pudding in years.'

He nodded. 'It didn't feel as if there was
much to celebrate. Lina, I had a head injury. It was six months of rehab and a year
before I went back to work, and once I was
back I chose to work over all the Christ-
mases and New Years. I've moved around
a lot since Carrie died, six months here, two
months there, I learned pretty quickly not

to tell anyone about it. There are too many questions, too many awkward glances and the assumption that I'm lonely or on the pull, and sometimes those assumptions were correct...' He was being very open. 'But then it was time to move on, and that meant taking a permanent position, which I have...' He looked over at Lina. 'I get what you mean about wanting your own place and putting down roots...'

'I've got a box at my mum's,' Lina said. 'I've never bothered unpacking it, but I will once I have my own place.'

'I never know what to do with our wedding photo, where to put it up, or if I should...'

'Of course you should.'

'It does tend to lead to an awful lot of questions,' Garth said.

Lina thought for a moment. His honesty was still so refreshing. She understood that a wedding photo on the wall wouldn't exactly help a fling or a short-term thing.

'I would have told you that morning,' Garth said, 'but then you walked out the door. Why?'

'Garth, I can't even make simple relationships work, let alone complicated ones.

I thought you were keeping things light with me, just putting on a front.'

'What on earth made you think that?'

'Lots of things. Carrie told me you and your dad don't get on, but you told me the two of you were close…'

'Ah…' Garth looked ahead now, perhaps glimpsing how confusing it had been. 'We didn't used to get on. My mother died when I was very young and if ever there was someone not cut out to be a single parent, it was him. He wanted his career and it was boarding school for me. I did have a time of it growing up, but when Carrie died he came into his own and was really supportive, and I suppose I gave him another chance. We get on better as two adults.'

'Is he in Wales?' she asked. 'Is that where you'd been when you brought those cakes back?'

'No, he's just outside London. It's her mother who's in Wales. I visit Gwen a couple of times a year. Carrie's father died a couple of months after the accident. Gwen's never got over it and I doubt she ever will.' He looked over. 'It's hell seeing her, because just when I'm feeling as if my life is moving on, I'm back again, going through albums and watching wedding videos and talking about grandchildren that can never be…'

Lina swallowed.

'Carrie was pregnant,' Garth told her, and it was such a relief that she wasn't the one telling him that. It was such a relief to let go of the stress of holding that knowledge and not knowing whether he knew. 'I wasn't supposed to know, but I'd seen the test and the champagne in the fridge…' He looked at her. 'Did she tell you?'

'Yes.' Lina started to cry, even though it wasn't quite her place to, but it was both a relief that he knew and she was so sad for what he had been through. And because she liked it that he cared about a lady who sat home alone with her memories.

'I do have one question,' he said, 'if you're okay answering it.'

She braced herself, and found that all the ropes holding her heart up were strong and intact.

'Was she scared?' Garth asked. 'I always worried that she was alone and scared.

'She wasn't scared.' Lina thought back and knew she had to be honest. 'Well, at first she was scared that she'd lost you, but you'd moved your arm and I told her I thought you could hear…' She let that sink in. 'Then she said she was worried about the baby…' Lina didn't look over to see his reaction, but she felt him squeeze her hand and gave his a squeeze back and then said, 'I told her we'd deal with the baby later and for now we were taking care of her…'

'Was she scared to die?' Garth asked. His voice was a husk and she could hear the years of dread and torment behind the words.

'I don't know that she knew she was,' Lina said. 'And I'm not making that up.' They looked at each other then. 'She was a doctor, I was a paramedic, so I guess we both knew, but it just… Somehow it was peaceful. She said she wasn't in pain and we talked right up to the end.' Lina said with certainty, 'She wasn't alone and she wasn't scared.'

They sat then for a moment, both lost in that night six years ago, both living it all over again.

'I understand why you couldn't tell me,' Garth said. 'For selfish reasons I didn't want you to have been there at the accident, and I'm not just talking about Carrie…'

'Then what?'

'I was embarrassed.'

She frowned, not understanding.

'I'm not now, but when you first told me, I hated that you'd seen me like that.'

Lina nodded, even though she had never thought of that until now, but a proud man like him would hate to have been seen rendered helpless. 'To be honest,' she said, 'I wasn't really paying much attention to you.'

They shared a very watery smile, but it helped dilute the pain of what they were discussing. 'Is there anything else you want to know?'

She held her breath, because she was scared, so scared that somehow he might blame her, that if he felt she'd not done enough, however misplaced, then it would surely be something they could never get past.

'I don't think so. I wish it hadn't been you but in the same thought I'm grateful that you were with her.'

They sat, listening to the whistle of the wind and the screeching of the gulls, but louder than that was the sound of her pulse in her ears as she waited for his polite smile and his careful words to thank her for laying his ghosts to rest.

To draw his neat conclusion and place a neat line under them.

For Garth to simply leave.

'Shall we walk?' he said, and Lina blinked. 'If we want to make it back before it starts getting dark…'

He was still here.

CHAPTER TWELVE

THINGS FELT LIGHTER when they started walking again. Though maybe, Lina conceded, that was because he was carrying her rucksack, but she felt her old self starting to filter back as her professional hat blew away with the wind.

'I need a drink,' Garth said as they huffed up a hill.

'I need an ice cream,' Lina said.

'It's freezing.'

'Then it won't melt.'

He laughed as they debated where they might eat in the village that would be home for the night. 'Come on,' he said. 'Almost there.'

They found a little Italian café and Lina got her ice cream and Garth had a ginger ale and cake. They sat outside in the thin winter sun, which was bracing but invigorating.

'So where are you staying?' Lina asked.

'There.' He pointed to the little hotel she had chosen for that night.

'It's the same one as me.'

'I know.' Garth smiled. 'I remembered you telling me about it and I decided to risk it...' He was honest. 'Lina, I can head back to London tonight if it's difficult for you. I know how much you've been looking forward to this and I really don't want to ruin your days off.'

'It's not difficult,' Lina responded. They were back to where they'd been, before she'd remembered—or even better than they'd been, because now there were no secrets between them. 'It is cold though. I think I'm going to check in and try to warm up in the shower.'

It was a lovely little hotel and she registered in a matter of moments and they headed to the stairs. 'Do you want to come up?' she offered. 'I believe there's a kettle *and* biscuits!'

Her room was gorgeous, if very small, but it looked out on the water. It was hard to believe he had come all this way just to speak to her.

'Thank you,' Lina said as she took off her huge jacket, 'for coming all this way to talk to me, for clearing the air...'

'It's the nicest walk I've ever had.'

'Really?' Lina frowned, doubting that it was.

'Really.' He took her wool and khaki-wrapped body in his arms and she was back in her favourite space, somewhere she'd never thought she'd be again. 'I don't think I've walked properly since camp at school.'

She laughed and then just rested a while in his arms.

'I've missed you,' Lina told him. 'I probably shouldn't admit that, but I've really missed you.'

'I've missed you too,' Garth said. 'I do have another question.'

'Oh!' She pulled back from his arms, not sure she was ready for what was to come.

'Would you ever have got in touch?'

'We'd have seen each other at work,' Lina said, attempting nonchalance for all of five seconds, but then giving in. 'Yes. I'd have probably caved and called you tonight, or...' She went in her rucksack and pulled out a scruffy paper bag. 'Failing that, I was going to give you this, with a card, though I haven't bought it yet...'

'What would the card say?'

'I don't know.'

'Try?'

'That I panicked,' Lina said, and took a breath.

'And…'

'That I'm not very used to relationships working out, and I thought that this might be too much, but I'd hoped…'

He opened the bag and took out the record she had brought. He frowned and smiled as he turned it over in his hands. 'Where the hell did you get this?'

'At a vintage shop. The man said it was really rare and I should snap it up. I don't know if he was just playing me.'

'He wasn't playing you, Lina…' He smiled. 'This is amazing, thank you.'

'You like it?'

'I love it.' He looked at her. 'You hate jazz.'

'You don't, though.'

'If you knew how sexy this was…' He held her and they danced around the little room, and she could almost hear the music she hadn't even known existed thrum through her body, making her less shy.

His kiss was like a gentle eraser, wiping all the fears and the troubles of the world away, a caress to her soul that felt almost familiar, as if it couldn't be any other way and could only be him in whose arms she unravelled.

He took off her ugly trousers, and massive black boots, shredding her armour in the process. Then he let out a low laugh when he saw her stunning satin burnt orange bra. 'That underwear you wore really wasn't for me...'

'Nope...'

Garth brushed back the hair from her face and kissed her deep and slow.

He was ruining her, Lina thought as they kissed, because she wanted long walks with him and kisses like this, and...for ever.

Her skin was all blotchy and cold and red and it was nice to jump into bed and lie under the heavy blankets and watch him undress. 'I'm so glad you're here.'

'I'm very pleased to be here too.'

Garth was far, far too big for her tiny bed, but it made it nicer somehow. It was deep in winter and so it was dark already, even though it was only late afternoon.

His skin was cold and his kiss warm, his hands taking in the curves of her body. That ease and excitement from before had returned.

He kissed her neck, and the roughness of his jaw as it dragged across her cheek caused her eyes to screw closed at the bliss as her mouth awaited his.

'Open them,' he said.

She looked into navy eyes as he told her that her eyes were the greenest he had ever seen. 'You're beautiful, Lina.'

She was so new to that feeling, and in his arms so accepting of it, because he made it true.

His kiss made her both shiver and burn. Her hand crept down his body, touching, caressing, until she held him again and stroked him between them.

Warm, intimate and tender, till they both needed more. He turned her onto her back and lifted up, just so that he could look down at her as they made love. She didn't care that her hair was a knotted mess and that her cheeks were pink from the wind.

She tasted the salty skin of his shoulder as they made tender love.

Nothing else mattered as they took themselves to a place only the other knew and she had to hold onto those three little words as she shattered beneath him, because otherwise she might end up telling him that at the age of almost thirty she had, for the first time, found love.

And it scared her.

He lay on top, both of them panting, catching their breaths as the world came back in, and all Lina knew was that she could never go back out there—could never venture back into single land if this didn't work out.

'What?' Garth asked as she rolled away, but he tucked her right in against him. 'You've gone all silent again.'

'I'm just...'

How she wanted to emergency-text Shona, or Brendan, or even May!

An emergency pow-wow was needed ASAP, except she had to make do with her own troubled mind.

It was too soon for declarations surely?

'Just what?' Garth prompted.

'Hungry,' she settled for instead.

'Then we'll go and get dinner...'

She swallowed and then turned and faced him, her deepest truth a whisper away.

'What's wrong?'

'I was going to grab some pasta at the Italian, well, that was my plan, but...' She had to be very honest now. 'Garth, I feel like I have the cheat sheet on you.'

'The cheat sheet?'

'That I could tick all your boxes because I know things about you, but I have to be me. It's tempting, though...'

'Lina, I have no idea what you're talking about.'

'Everyone keeps telling me what I'm doing wrong, how I need to be less assertive, wear a dress, be more this, less that...' They lay facing each other in the cocoon of bedding as she bared her soul. 'I want to keep you,' she admitted, 'and I'm scared I might use my superpower for evil. I live in jeans, I love pasta, I hate jazz. Remember the cat thing?'

'Lina,' he broke in, 'can I tell you something.'

She nodded.

'Carrie knew a different me.' There was a huskiness to his voice that told Lina how difficult these words were to say. 'And while I did used to say that I hate pasta, I would kill to sit and have the biggest bowl with her...'

She nodded, because that much she understood.

'The little things that once seemed to matter don't any more when you lose someone you love.'

'I guess.'

'It's true, because I guard my privacy more than anyone, but after you'd gone, I sat in the office and I spoke with May...'

'You told May?'

'I couldn't just keep on working.'

'Because of Carrie...' she said, running

a hand through his thick dark hair, just so honest and warm and safe in this bed.

'Because of Carrie and because of you. May pretty much knew most of it anyway— she was on the interview panel after all, but I ended up telling her about you...'

It was the nicest break of confidence she had ever heard, that this gorgeous man had opened up to someone about her.

'I'd love to share a bowl of pasta with you, Lina.'

She smiled, and then laughed. 'Do you know what, I don't even fancy it now...' She could hear the rain battering the window now. 'Shall we just get something sent up?'

'How about you let me take care of dinner?' Garth said. 'I could book us a table downstairs.'

'A *date* date?' Lina checked.

'Why do you think I'm here, Lina?'

To find out about Carrie, to resurrect them, to see if they were salvageable...but then he said something that made her heart go completely still, 'I'm here to fight for us.'

'Fight for us?'

'Yes...' He looked at her very seriously. 'I know we could have done things differently, on both sides, but I'm not going to let something as wonderful as we've found slip away…'

His words made her shake.

In fact, they were the words she had waited for ever to hear.

Someone who fought for her.

Fought for them.

Didn't just give up when things got too hard or too messy. Didn't just up sticks and walk away.

Except he was climbing out of bed. 'Where are you going?'

'To get ready,' Garth said. 'I'll meet you down there at, say, seven…?'

Lina nodded as she silently panicked.

She had a *date* date. A serious, proper date with a man she was—whisper—in love with, and who was possibly starting to feel the same, and she had *absolutely* nothing to wear.

There was no Shona and her wardrobe of many colours to draw on.

No high street to dash out to.

Nothing.

She gulped as she thought of May's words: 'We'll just have to work with what we've got.'

Not much!

There was her interview dress, but this

wasn't an interview, because the questions had all been asked and answered.

And so she put on jeans but wore the nice black jumper she had worn for her interview and put on lip balm and wore her hair down.

That *was* Lina making an effort.

Apart from the violet dress, Lina realised, he hadn't seen her in anything other than her uniform or practical walking clothes, or bundled up in a coat and scarf.

And yet, she reminded herself, he still liked her.

He didn't seem to mind the wet and messy hair, and that she talked about work, and he didn't even seem to mind her egg sandwiches.

She was nervous. Like one of his awful jazz songs, her heart was going *boop-doop, doop-doop* as she made her way down the creaking steps of the little hotel, following the herby scents to the bar.

And there, waiting for her, standing up as she entered, like the old-fashioned guy he was, was Garth.

He wore black jeans, a black jumper, and he'd actually shaved.

'You look so handsome,' she said, and caught a whiff of cologne as they shared a brief kiss.

'You look stunning,' he told her, and the blaze in his eyes told her he meant every word. That this version of Lina was better than fine by him.

'Thank you.'

She was embarrassed, shy and pleased all at the same time.

She felt feminine and herself as they sat by a roaring fire in a pub, both drinking beer, Lina ordering crab on toast and him ordering an amazing-sounding pie that was topped with blue cheese.

And between mouthfuls and a little taste of each other's food and a whole lot of laughter, they talked.

They talked about Gretel's diabetes—and his eyes didn't glaze over. In fact, he took it just as seriously as he would if the cat were a patient, which delighted Lina.

She told him about her model vintage ambulance collection and he discussed in great depth his vast vinyl collection—her eyes did glaze a little, but that was possibly lust or the stronger-than-expected beer. And how warm the flat was, thanks to her radiator skills. But he still needed...

'Curtains,' Lina finished for him.

'Yes!'

'We know all this stuff about each other...'

'Except we know so little.' Garth smiled. 'I can't wait to get to know you some more, Lina.'

'I can't wait to get to know you either.' She smiled back and thought about it and then said it again. 'I honestly can't. I've never felt like this before, Garth. In fact…' She blushed at her own presumption. 'What are you doing next weekend?'

'Working. Why?'

'It doesn't matter.'

'Why?' Garth pushed.

She was finally brave, because his hand on her thigh made her so. 'Alison and Brendan have asked me to be godmother and they said I can bring someone… It's not a big deal.' She corrected herself. 'I mean, it's a big deal that they've asked me, but it's fine that you can't make it…'

'I'd love to be there.'

'Really?'

'I am down to be working,' he admitted. 'I actually had to swap things around to get these days off, but I'm sure I can sort something out with Richard…' He took out his phone and put in the date; it was just about the nicest thing he could have done for her. 'I'll do my best to be there, even if I can only get away for the service.'

That he would try meant the world. 'Thank you,' she said. It made a special day extra special.

'Lina, about you telling me at work...'

She felt her hopes suddenly plummet, as though the cable on a lift had snapped, Maybe he'd decided to ditch her in public and, no, she wasn't being dramatic. Lina had had two men disappear on her mid-dinner.

'You were right to...'

'Right?'

'Would Alison wait till Brendan's shift ended to let him know she was in labour?'

'No.'

'Life happens in real time,' Garth said, 'and I want my life to happen with you in it. I never thought I'd be happy again,' Garth told her. 'Not truly. And I don't mean that in a depressing way. Hell, I have a nice life, I just never thought I'd feel *it* again.'

'It?' Lina checked, because that was exactly how she herself had described it, this feeling that had descended the second she had walked into the staffroom and seen him.

The awareness that had knocked the breath from her when she had first taken a seat by his side.

But, more than that, it was the confidence he gave her and the acceptance, the moments of being herself, shared with someone who felt *it* too, enough to address the parts that hurt. 'I know you'll always miss her.'

'Yes,' Garth said. 'And I miss life for her, if that makes sense, but you make me happy, Lina, in a way I never expected to feel again.' He was serious all of a sudden. 'Lina,' he said, 'I can't get through dinner without asking. Will you marry me, please?'

'Pardon?'

'I know I should have a ring, but we can go and choose one together…'

'You want me to marry you?'

'Yes, please.'

'Me?'

'Yes you.'

'But we're only on our…' she counted '…second date. Or third if you count break-fast.'

'I don't need another to know I love you.'

'I love you too.' It was, as it turned out, as simple as that. 'I love you, Garth.' It was a relief to say it, to admit it, to kiss and con-firm it, but there was just one thing weigh-ing on her mind. 'You don't have to marry me, though. We can live together, we can—'

He pulled his face back, but held it in his palms. 'What aren't you telling me?'

Lina took a breath and looked into the

dark pools of his eyes and knew that with this man she really could be honest. 'I don't want a big wedding. I don't want...' she made herself say it '...to ask my father and have him not come, or...' she swallowed '...if he does, expect it to be big, given he's come all that way...'

'Lina,' he said. 'Do *you* want to marry me?'

'More than anything in the world.'

'And do you want a big wedding?'

'It's just not me.'

'Fine,' Garth said, 'then we'll have a tiny wedding but, Lina Edwards, I am going to marry you!'

CHAPTER THIRTEEN

'ANY PLANS FOR your days off?'

'None,' Lina said, and to avoid meeting Brendan's eyes she looked out of the window. 'Well, I'm moving the last of my stuff into Garth's.'

'You two really are serious, then?'

'We really are.' She turned now and smiled. 'What are you up to?'

'We're moving Michael into his own room,' Brendan said. 'I'm setting up the monitor tonight.'

It was a busy shift and they ended up at The Primary at ten p. m. when they should have been signing off. 'I thought you finished at nine,' Lina said when she saw May.

'No rest for the wicked,' May muttered. 'Still, I can't complain. I've got the weekend away from this madhouse...'

Just another weekend, except Lina could

not wait, because tomorrow—not that anyone apart from her and Garth knew—she would become Mrs Lina Hughes.

She felt a little guilty about not sharing her news with Brendan, but if she did, she'd only feel more guilty for not telling her mum and brothers, and if she told them it would mean telling her dad, who she was sure wouldn't come. Then there was Garth's dad and his new lady friend…

It would all get too complicated for words and so they had decided to keep it to themselves for now.

She crept into the flat at eleven and tried to ignore the Shona and Marcus love fest going on in the next room as she put on a face pack and did her nails.

'What are you up to?' Shona asked when they met in the hallway past midnight.

'I'm just having a shower to wash this conditioner out.'

It was exhausting being polished and elegant!

They'd gone shopping, but Lina had decided she didn't want an engagement ring. 'I'd have to take it off for work and I know I'd lose it…' And as well as that, they wanted to keep their secret a little while longer from the world.

So, instead of shopping for an engagement ring, they'd headed to the blacksmiths in Gretna Green and bought wedding bands that fitted together with the anvil mark hidden on the inside.

They weren't eloping exactly, but it came pretty close.

The morning of the wedding loomed and Shona headed off for her shift at the beauty clinic. When Lina safely had the place to herself, the *real* preparations began.

Using curling tongs, Lina livened up her hair and then did her make-up, as she did on occasion now. With the clock running away with itself, she cut all the labels and price tags out of her very expensive silk underwear and put it on.

This set of underwear was for him.

Well, for her too, but she couldn't wait to see his smile when he saw the gorgeous white velvet and tiny red bows. It was subtle—virginal sexy—and just so gorgeous that it was worth an entire Saturday night shift at The Primary.

The set had cost more than her dress.

Ah, but what a dress.

It was a gorgeous crisp white cotton embroidered with red roses and she had known the second she'd seen it that this was the one.

She slipped it on and struggled to do up the tiny zip at the back and then slipped into the heels she had worn for Michael's christening last week.

Garth was waiting for her, and walked towards her as she stepped out of the taxi.

It was a gorgeous registry office, beside parks and a river. It was a busy Saturday in London but here it was peaceful as they walked hand in hand to make their vows.

'Oh, Lina,' he said, because over and over she amazed him and in turn he took her breath away, for he wore a charcoal-grey suit and a grey tie with a shirt as crisp and white as the cotton on her dress.

'I'm terrified,' Lina admitted.

'But sure?' Garth checked.

'I have never been so sure of anything in my life.'

'You look beautiful,' Garth said, and he kissed her on the cheek so as not to spoil her lipstick, and, still hand in hand, they walked in together when their names were called.

The celebrant was glamorous indeed, with caramel-blonde hair and a stunning suit, and it made the day just a little more special to see her smile and the effort she had made.

'Just the two of you?' she asked as the seats in the room remained empty and they had their two borrowed witnesses.

'Just us.' Garth smiled.

'That's all a marriage needs,' the celebrant said, and the formalities began.

The ring felt heavy and cool as Garth slipped it on her finger, but how right it felt to be wearing it, Lina thought.

And she looked at his expression as he examined his white-gold ring. There was that second, she knew, when he must have been thinking about the first time, but it wasn't a threat to her, just a poignant moment that meant they both knew how lucky they were to have found each other.

'You are now husband and wife.'

His kiss was thorough and her lipstick, along with her heart, was completely gone as she gazed at her husband and smiled.

They had hired a photographer to take a few pictures on a little bridge outside, and they headed there to stand amidst the geese and swans.

Except there, waiting for them, was the biggest surprise.

Trefor Hughes and his lady friend, as well as Lina's mum and her brothers, Richard and May and a few others from The Primary, and she hoped no one needed help because it seemed that half of her paramedic colleagues just happened to be there, having a picnic!

'She's got legs!' Brendan shouted as Lina stood, stunned, and everyone laughed.

'You did this!' Lina gaped and then turned to Garth. 'How on earth…?'

'I had nothing to do with this. In fact, I had absolutely no idea,' Garth said, staring in bemusement at the activities taking place. Blankets were being spread on the grass and corks were popping. Shona was there, with Marcus in tow. 'There's Boris…' Garth said, pointing to a man arriving with a wicker picnic basket and another wrapped gift that could possibly be more bubble bath and candles.

'Lina…' Her mum embraced her. 'I am so happy for you and…' she looked at her new son-in-law '… Garth, it's lovely to meet you.'

'It's lovely to meet you too, Jeanette.'

Her mum pulled Lina aside the first chance she got.

'You don't mind that we didn't tell you?' Lina checked.

'Of course not. I dreaded a big wedding and having to face your dad again and…'

She rolled her eyes. 'He was asked, of course, but he was never going to come all this way for a picnic...'

It was the only teeny blot on a wonderful day. But then he called and it felt like the best gift.

'Congratulations!' her dad said. 'Your colleague Brendan called me on Wednesday. If I'd known earlier, I'd have tried—'

'Dad, it's fine, I didn't even know they were sorting out a party.' They chatted a little, and he even spoke to Garth before they returned to their surprise party.

There were nieces and nephews and Michael lying there, kicking his legs, and Brendan happily confided that of course he'd guessed that she was up to something.

'Alison took Michael out for the day and checked the marriage notices on display...' Brendan laughed. 'We thought it would take ages, but it was the first registry office she went to,' he said, proud of himself and his wife for carrying it off.

'How did you know?'

'Because I've never seen you so happy,' Brendan said, 'and I've never known you so reluctant to talk. I knew you were up to something.'

Of course he had.

Lina had known she had wonderful friends and that even during the lonelier times they had, in their own unique ways, all been there for her.

They were certainly here for her now, doing everything they could to make today an extra-special one.

There were egg sandwiches, of course, but they were cut in little triangles, and instead of tuna it was smoked salmon and cream cheese, and Les thoroughly approved of them.

There were little lemon meringue pies and scones with cream and jam and just the most gorgeous afternoon tea, spread out on the lawn with all the people they cared about and loved, and who cared about and loved them in return.

'You didn't think we'd let you get off without a little party, now, did you?' May said, pouring champagne. 'You're one of us.'

There were no speeches, no pressure, just love and laughter on a lazy spring afternoon, with children running and adults laughing. If she had arranged this party herself it could not have been more perfect.

And later, as the blankets were all cleared away and the happy crowd drifted off, ev-

eryone agreed it had been a brilliant wedding.

'You've got grass in your hair,' Garth said
as he picked it out on the taxi ride home.

'Here,' he said, and handed her a gorgeous
keyring and a key of her own. As she turned
the key in the lock, Lina didn't get to step
into her new home, instead he swept her
up and she laughed as he carried her from
room to room.

The lounge room windows had long,
heavy amber velvet drapes, and the ones in
the huge spare room were jade-green and
in the bedroom, well, they were kingfisher-
blue…

Then he put her down by their brand-new
dressing table, where a bottle of champagne
was cooling in an ice bucket. Leaning on it
was an envelope.

Mrs Lina Hughes

'What's this?' Lina asked, turning the envelope over in her hands and looking for
clues as to what it contained.

'It's our wedding present.'

Lina frowned and felt a little flurry of
panic, because she hadn't got him any-

thing. Well, there was the underwear, but that didn't count! 'I didn't get us anything.'

'Just open it, Lina.'

She peeled open the envelope and took out a smart navy wallet, and then swallowed when she saw that it was two plane tickets to Singapore as well as a booking for ten nights in a rather nice hotel.

'Singapore?' She blinked and just stared at the tickets that would carry her towards a father she wasn't sure wanted her, one who might make excuses as to why he couldn't fit her in. And almost pre-empting that, she started to make them on her father's behalf... 'What if he's working or—?'

'I'm sure we can have lunch with him,' Garth said. 'Or dinner...'

'But what if—?'

'I said on the phone that I'm looking forward to meeting him, and he said the same.'

It was such a relief to hear someone speak nicely about her father—always it felt as if he was being criticised, yet Garth seemed to instinctively get that it simply didn't help matters. Still, as exciting as the prospect was, there was that nagging dread that, despite his words to the contrary, her father might not be so thrilled at the thought of spending time with her. 'What if he doesn't want me back in his life, Garth?'

'Then I'll take you to the rooftop bar and we can drown our sorrows in Singapore slings.' Garth smiled. 'But I'm sure that won't be necessary.' He could see that she wasn't convinced and though he couldn't be positive of the outcome, he knew one thing for sure. 'Lina, I get on with my father now a thousand times better than I did growing up. You're already ahead of me there. He gave you a great childhood...'

'He did.'

'And then the teenage years got all messed up, but I'm sure you can sort it out...'

He sounded so positive. He was a living example after all, and it helped to know that when she got off that plane in Singapore it would be with Garth beside her, and at that awkward first meeting with him Garth would be there too.

Maybe he was right. Maybe this really could be the start of a whole new relationship with her family on the other side of the world.

'I'll call him and tell him we're coming,' she said with a smile.

'Call him tomorrow,' Garth said, and she nodded and smiled again.

She frowned at an old gramophone and then laughed as he took out a familiar-looking old record.

'Am I going to ruin your night by playing jazz?' Garth said as he lowered the needle onto the record.

It was slow and melodious and beat into her blood as it danced through her veins.

He pulled down her zipper and kissed her shoulder as he peeled off her bra. 'I think white drapes for the bathroom,' he whispered, 'with little red bows.'

'Of course,' she replied.

He had made his home theirs, each room already holding a memory…

EPILOGUE

BRENDAN HAD BEEN RIGHT.

Lina would never, ever tell him that, of course, but the fact was Brendan had been right when he'd said that being a parent changed everything!

Martha Aileen Hughes had been born six months ago but she'd changed their lives long before that.

Lina had been working in the control room since she'd found out that she was pregnant and had been on maternity leave since she'd had her daughter, but she was returning part time and was back in the driving seat for the first time in what felt like for ever.

'Here…' Garth said, and handed her a lunchbox from the fridge, filled with egg sandwiches, a chocolate bar and a muffin, as she squeezed a last cuddle out of Martha before she headed off.

She was adorable.

Fat cheeks, fat hands and the biggest blue eyes, and a single black curl on the top of an otherwise bald head. She had them both besotted.

On her first shift back from maternity leave they were called out to an eight-month-old with respiratory distress and it was blue lights all the way to The Primary.

'Lina!' May said as she came in with mum on the stretcher holding the baby.

Except there wasn't time for a catch-up or to share photos of Martha, because one look at the baby and May was waving them through to Resus. 'Richard!' May called in a voice Lina knew only too well.

He was there in seconds, examining the little baby as Lina guided the shaky mother to Reception to register the babe.

Lina felt shaky herself.

Back in the ambulance she let out a breath. 'Nice work,' Brendan said, and then looked at her. 'The baby will be fine.'

'I know.' Lina nodded, because she'd already started to look better by the time they'd left. 'But Martha's cheeks were a bit red when I left and there's loads going around...'

'I'm sure Garth would call if there were any issues,' Brendan said.

'Of course he would.'

'And he is a doctor,' Brendan pointed out. 'Martha couldn't be with anyone more qualified…'

'I know all that.' Lina sighed.

'That baby was sick,' Brendan said patiently. 'Martha's just teething.'

'I know all that, it's just…' She rolled her eyes and gave in. 'It's different when you have one of your own.'

'Told you so!' Brendan couldn't help himself but after a triumphant smile he was kind. 'Maybe text him and check everything's okay.'

'It's two in the morning.'

So rather than wake Garth, she breathed her way through the rest of her shift, and chatted with Brendan about, well, everything really.

Well, not *everything*.

It had been on their honeymoon that Martha had been conceived, she and Garth were sure.

They had explored Bukit Timah Nature Reserve with her father and his family, and they'd been on a night safari with them too. And while it might not sound romantic to spend half your honeymoon with your long-lost dad and his family, it had been magical for Lina. And because it was their honeymoon, she and Garth had been on river cruises and, yes, there had been Singapore slings. It had been such a magical time they had decided they would soon come back for another visit.

This time with little Martha in tow.

Garth still drove over to Wales now and then and Lina stayed behind. It was bittersweet for Carrie's mum, of course, but she was a kind and gracious lady and had sent a card and a little knitted cardigan for Martha, which she would be wearing for her christening...

Speaking of which...

'Do you and Alison want to come for dinner next week, or lunch?' Lina invited, oh, so casually.

'Lunch would be better,' Brendan said. 'Michael's on a strict schedule...' He turned and smiled. 'Any reason?'

'No reason.' Lina smiled. Other than that they would be asking Brendan to be godfather, and they were also going to ask May to be godmother. 'It would just be nice to catch up out of work.'

It felt good to be back. But for Lina it had

been a very long night and she simply could not wait to be home, and she wasn't relishing the long journey ahead.

Sometimes Garth just got it so right, because at the end of her first shift, when she was ready to dive into the tube, and itching, just clawing, to see for herself that Martha was okay, there he was, standing by the car with a takeout coffee for her, and undoubtedly a tea for him, and a paper bag, which she rightly guessed held almond croissants.

'How was your shift?' he asked.

'Long,' Lina said. 'It was good, though.'

But there was something she wanted far more than croissants and coffee for there, in the back, nestled in her little car seat, was a sleeping Martha.

Her little hands were sticking out of the blanket, the fingers splayed as if in surprise, and she was the sweetest sight for sore, tired eyes.

'She woke up at two and then at five,' Garth explained, 'and then wouldn't settle.'

'Do you think she missed me?'

'She did, but then she decided that I'd have to do and took her bottle, but rather than go back to sleep she decided to practise chewing her feet.' He laughed.

It was so brilliant to see his smile and to

hear his laugh. Such a privilege to see the happiness return to his world and lightness revive his heart.

'Did you give Gretel her treats?'

'Yes, I gave Gretel her treats,' he said. 'She missed you too.' They drove home, chatting about each other's nights, then he parked the car and took the lift up to the apartment. He carried Martha as Lina wanted to shower before she had a much-needed cuddle with her daughter.

She turned the key and had to pause for a second for she just loved stepping into her home.

Their home.

Her own boxes had finally been unpacked and there, amongst the med-school pictures and their graduation and holiday photos and childhoods and their wedding photo, was another one…

The past wasn't hidden, and when Martha asked who the other gorgeous bride was, they would tell her, of course.

It brought a lump to Lina's throat this morning as she passed.

She went straight to the shower, where she shed her uniform and came out wrapped in towels to the sight of Martha asleep in her cot and Garth undressed and back in bed.

Sunday morning breakfast with Garth really was the nicest treat in the world and they lay there, sharing kisses and conversation and eating their treats.

Safe in love.

* * * * *

*If you enjoyed this story, check out
these other great reads from
Carol Marinelli*

The Nurse's Reunion Wish
The Surgeon's Gift
Emergency at Bayside
Accidental Reunion

All available now!